RELENTLESS

MIKE MCCRARY

For Polly

"No adultery is bloodless."
-- Natalia Ginzburg

PART I

1

───────

"Not good."

Davis Briggs talks on his phone while pacing in small circles. He moves, pauses, pivots and moves again, working the pavement in front of the Viceroy hotel in Santa Monica. The place is buzzing. He carries on his anxious conversation slightly to the right side of the valet stand, away from the beautiful throngs that reside in and frequent Westside Los Angeles.

His eyes take in everything around him. His ears soak up the tension from the phone call. Ridiculously priced cars come and go with the attractive folks of LA drifting back and forth, passing by while paying Davis no mind. An invisible man among people who are hard to look away from.

The uncomfortable conversation he's having is

with his business partner, and Davis's discomfort is only compounded by his feeling of being discounted by good-looking, wealthier people. Their eyes look everywhere but at him. Purposeful in the casual way they ignore an ordinary man. Spending their focus elsewhere, looking to see who's looking at them. Who they need to see. Davis might as well be homeless with a tattered paper cup begging for their spare change.

He isn't an unattractive man. No disfiguring scars. Not overweight. Not in Olympic shape either. He's someone you went to high school with. Someone who lives down the street. A dad at your kid's school. But certainly not an underwear model. He couldn't begin to tell you his daily grams of protein intake.

His crime tonight is being average.

Ordinary.

And ordinarily, average isn't what hangs out at this hotel.

Big-money suits strut by. Shabby-chic hipsters roll. Genetically fortunate women wearing impossibly tight dresses that cling to their heavenly bodies glide in and out of this hotel, and all of them come armed with loose wallets ready to vomit cash and credit. All this high net worth mass of gorgeous is what's steaming past Davis like water rolling over a simple stone stuck at the bottom of a creek.

"What do you mean by 'not good'?" his business partner Todd asks.

Davis is out of place. Out of his league, stuck in a game he's unfamiliar with.

His clothes give him away, right away. He's dressed like a guy who's trying hard to play the part of a big-time businessman, only on a penny-pincher's budget. Mid-priced pants and shirt that don't fit all that well, along with shoes that are south of their prime. Not horrible, nothing necessarily wrong with what he has on, but his garb is far from custom, and its total cost is miles away from anyone else within a mile of this place.

He untucked his shirt an hour ago but doesn't feel comfortable with it.

A man in a three-thousand-dollar suit knocks into Davis without offering an apology. Davis glances toward him as he takes a stumbling step backward, but doesn't look long. Avoids eye contact. Avoids confrontation.

Stay in your lane, Davis.

"Look, man, I'm sorry." Davis returns to his phone conversation. "I didn't want to come here anyway."

"I can't be in two places at once. We're not a huge shop," Todd says. "We gotta sell. Last I heard that's how revenue gets generated."

"Yeah, I know how revenue works."

"Do you?"

"Stop." Davis rubs his face, watches a Bentley pull away.

"It couldn't have gone that bad, right?" Todd pauses. "Right?"

Davis grits his teeth in silence, looking to the night sky for some assistance.

"Shit. It was. It was that bad, wasn't it?" Todd says. "Oh Jesus, tell me it wasn't that bad."

"It wasn't great," Davis says, glancing toward his feet. Even while on the phone he can't look Todd in the eye. The weight of letting down his business partner is crushing. The feeling that he's letting his friend down fringes on unbearable.

A woman bumps into him. Davis bounces back then apologizes but doesn't know why.

"Let's talk about it when I get back," Davis tells Todd.

"Tell me what happened. What did they say?" Todd starts up again.

"I've still got one more meeting tomorrow. I'll make it work." Even as it comes out of his mouth Davis doesn't believe it.

"Davis. Talk to me, man. What. Happened?"

A beautiful woman catches Davis's eye. Her eyes slip toward him. She looks straight at him, lets her eyes take him in. She's not looking at him in the same way as the others. For starters, she's looking at him. Only him. Locked in. Not looking away at all. She smiles. There's a warmth to her, a wanting to connect with him. All but simply asking him to talk to her.

Davis freezes.

"Hi," she says.

Davis allows a smile but doesn't say anything.

"So shy," she says as she passes by. "Like that. Like that a lot."

2

"Davis, what in the holy hell happened in that meeting?"

Todd is getting exhausted from dragging it out of his friend.

Davis snaps back to the here and now, turning away from the woman as she disappears into the hotel. He clears his throat. "They said we're creating a solution to a problem that doesn't exist."

Now there's silence on Todd's side of the phone. Not normal.

"Todd?"

"We're hearing this shit more and more."

"I know."

"You hear it once, fine. You hear it over and over?"

"They're wrong."

"Okay, I hear you. I appreciate the confidence,

but after a while you gotta think maybe we're the ones getting it wrong."

Davis closes his eyes, thinks of getting into it for the thousandth time with Todd, but stops himself. His phone bails him out with a beep.

HATTIE, the screen reads. His wife.

"Gotta go," Davis says.

"What? The hell you do."

"It's Hattie."

"Dammit." You can hear Todd's eyes roll. "Call me back."

"Of course."

"I mean it."

Davis flips over to Hattie. "Hi."

"Hey, how's it going?"

Davis cringes from the concern in her voice. They had such a hopeful conversation last night before he left town. She knows everything. Knows about the struggles the business is having. Letting her down is ten times more crushing than Todd. He can't go through this same conversation again, not now, not with her.

"It's okay. Making some progress. Got one more meeting in the morning, but it looks good."

"Okay. Great. That has to make you feel better."

Davis swallows hard. Hates lying to her, even if it's done to make them both feel better.

"Right? You feel better?" she asks.

"Yeah, it helps."

"So you'll be back tomorrow?"

"Yeah, I'm catching a flight after the meeting. Should be back by dinner."

"How's the hotel? I know it's not the Viceroy, but I hope it's okay."

Davis stares at the Viceroy sign covered in light. Hates himself even more. He thinks about their talk before he left home. About how they couldn't afford a place like that. Not the Viceroy. They decided he could stay a couple of blocks over and save a few bucks. That place down the road is still expensive as hell, but not insane like the Viceroy.

He'd argued it was the conference hotel and they had to look like they belonged.

You can't fool these people, he said. *You have to look the part*, he explained.

She talked about how they have to be careful with money this time around. How they needed to be smarter and patient, at least until the business took off. They got lucky and survived the last time around, but things are different now. The last time, Davis pushed their family to the brink of financial disaster. Hattie would never use those words, she's better than that, and would never pin any of that on Davis because they are in this together, but he knows the truth. At least he thinks he does. His projection of the truth at least

He feels the weight of every failure.

They agreed they'd play it safe until Davis and Todd's software company got rolling. She knows it will, even when Davis doesn't, but they need to treat it like a marathon. Not a sprint.

He reviews the rest of the *talk* that quickly escalated to a fight.

He travels too much.

She works too much.

The kids are driving them insane.

Money stress.

Work stress.

The house needs work.

Her parents.

His father.

The girls.

Money.

The same old ground they've stomping over and over again recently. He's starting to feel like he can script the arguments before they happen. He joked one time that he would hire someone to run the lines next time they fought. She laughed, then told him they couldn't afford that. It was funny. That's their relationship, love with sparring, but Davis took it as a true jab intended to leave a mark.

"Hotel's fine." Davis quickly changes the subject. "The girls still awake?"

"They're getting ready for bed." She takes a

beat to choose her words. "You okay? You sound off."

"I'm fine."

She always could spot the hint of bullshit from him.

From the corner of his eye Davis sees the same jaw-dropping woman from before, but this time she's with a slick-looking man who seems like he was peeled away from a film set. Perfect face. Perfect hair. Fit body in a suit cut just for him.

Davis stares. There's an undeniable energy flowing between them. They smile and laugh, wrapped around each other. Two beautiful people standing out in a crowd of beautiful people. Davis can't keep his eyes off of them.

They turn and look to Davis, then smile.

"You don't sound fine," Hattie says with a sweetness only she can bring.

Davis shakes it off. "I'm just tired."

"You sure?"

"Yeah."

"Would you tell me if it was something else?"

"Yes. Jesus, Hattie. I'm fine."

There's a cold silence. Davis realizes he put too much bite on his words. Davis looks up. The beautiful woman and man are gone.

"Okay," she finally says. "I'm going to go check on the girls."

"Hattie—"

She's already hung up.

"Dammit," he mutters to himself.

Davis pockets his phone, then retreats through the front doors of the hotel and into the lobby. He can't help but think the lights hanging from the ceiling cost more than his house. Hand-carved hardwood floors are peppered with white leather chairs filled with more of the pretty people from outside. They sip cocktails. They fake laughs. Fake flashing smiles filled with the whitest teeth he's ever seen.

There's a muted thump of bass seeping into the lobby. Davis looks toward the bar to his right, considers it. Thinks hard about grabbing a drink, could really use one, but decides better of it. Adding booze to his already delicate equation might not be the best decision right now. Not to mention, he's got that one last meeting tomorrow. Perhaps his last, if it doesn't turn out better than the ones today. He takes the elevator up to his room. He knows it's the right thing to do, but he's not happy with himself.

The silence is deafening inside his room, but he likes it in a way.

His shoulders come down from their usual arched position near his ears. He can feel his back loosen. He feels like he can breathe a little easier in here. The room is nicer than nice. Everything is new, polished and shines to perfection. Every detail handpicked by people who know how to handpick these sorts of things. Davis knows he's not one of those people, but he loves the fact those people are out there in the world.

There's a slight thought about money; it's been at least five minutes since he's thought about money, after all. The cost of this room sticks in his brain like a planted flag claiming territory, but Davis pushes it all down almost immediately. What's done is done. Can't get out of this room now.

He appreciates the finer things. Can't afford them, but likes them all the same. Pulling back the curtain, Davis steals a look out the window. He watches all the cars and limos come and go from the parking lot. Can't help but think about the lives being lived in those vehicles. The size of the bank accounts of the people inside. The money from simply selling one of those vehicles would solve all of Davis's money problems.

Money doesn't buy happiness, it's true, but it does take care of the vast majority of stress most people carry around day in and day out. That cannot be argued.

The number one thing he and Hattie fight about is money. They love each other, care about each other, but Davis knows what marriage can do to people over time. Despite what some say, being married is about more than love. You become a small company with projects and tasks, and those usually have a price tag. The difference, however, between marriage and a company is a big one.

Love.

Love helps keep it together when marriage inc. is deep in the red.

Davis sits on the side of the bed letting his head unwind. Trying to undo the conversations he had downstairs. Unspool the talks with Todd and Hattie. Hoping to find a reset button.

His black workbag rests against the wall. His presentation pitch book pokes out, just enough peeking above the zipper to tease and mock him. Calling him out while ever so quietly reminding him of today's business missteps. Just enough to pull him deeper into his troubled head.

He debates standing up and grabbing his bag so he can review the pitch. Review it again, one more time, see if there is something he could do better than he did today. A point he could make clearer. A data point he glossed over last time. A better way to say or explain something that didn't land well. Find something that will get them to sign on the line that is dotted.

He knows there isn't. He's not good at this. He's not Todd. He balls up his fists. Shuts his eyes tight. The frustration swells. He can't hold back what's flooding into his brain. Failure is coming. He can't stop it. He knows it. He grits his teeth.

The money.
The sales.
The business.
The dream is failing.
Again.

Davis slams his fist into the wall. The dull thump vibrates throughout the room. The light above sways ever so slightly. A black and white picture of a wave crashing into the shore drops to the floor. His eyes pop open as the crunch echoes.

The glass has cracked into a spiderweb.

"Shit."

3

———

Davis carves through the lobby.

He's back downstairs, working, worming his way through the members of LA's elite and those wanting to make you *believe* they're elite.

After breaking the picture in his room, Davis decided he needed something to smooth his edges. He splashed some water on his face, changed his clothes, and came back downstairs to be among the people enjoying the fashionable Santa Monica hotel. He bobs and weaves, making a path through the crowded Viceroy's lobby in search of a drink.

Something to smooth out his edges, all right.

More edges forming by the second.

Not an easy task, but he finds a spot at the bar. It's still early for an LA night, so it's not completely insane. You can still somewhat hear yourself think, but the party is only starting to swell. Won't be long before the music and the crowd will overtake the senses. Like ants spreading over a carcass.

A bartender slides over toward Davis. Chiseled good looks, more than likely an undiscovered talent, but still seems annoyed as hell he has to do his job.

"Can I get a whiskey?" Davis asks.

"What kind, boss?"

Davis scans the bottles. Most he doesn't know, but he sees one. He sees a good one. One he considers a good one at least. One he'd never order out with his wife. It's beer and wine when they go out, which is hardly ever, and it's usually a chain near the house. It's easier than driving into downtown Portland. They'd like to do more downtown, but closer to home takes less time, so they can pay the sitter less.

"Knob Creek?" Davis asks.

His phone buzzes. It's Todd.

Davis rolls his eyes as he answers. "Yeah."

"Were you going to call me back?"

"I just got off the phone with Hattie," Davis says like he's been dragged for miles. He feels his shoulders inch back up toward his ears. "Be nice to me."

"I didn't tell you to get married."

"Don't. It's not her, she's right—"

"Tab?" the bartender asks, sliding a glass of whiskey in front of him.

"No, just the one. How much?" He takes a sip.

"Fifteen."

Davis chokes, almost spits his whiskey all over the bar. "A glass?"

"It's single barrel," the bartender says while staring at a passing woman's enhanced chest.

Pulling out a crumpled twenty, Davis reluctantly slides his money over. The bartender snatches it up. Davis doesn't expect to see any change come back his way. He hears Todd giggle through the phone. Davis almost forgot he was there.

"Enjoying LA?" Todd asks.

"No."

"Drink your fifteen-dollar whiskey, slowly I recommend, and let's talk some business. Or, if you prefer, I'll talk and you drink."

Davis drinks. He'd rather talk about anything but business, and he'd sure as hell rather not hear Todd talk about it. Fresh out of options, he says, "Sure."

"What's the plan here, man? Our runway is getting shorter by the day. This isn't why we started this. The idea was to be happier."

"I know."

"I can make that call we talked about."

Davis's eyes flare. He knows what call Todd is talking about. Hattie wasn't the only fight Davis had before he left.

"Let me make the call," Todd presses. "What can it hurt to hear them out?"

"No. We've got this," Davis says, trying to convince himself. "We don't have to—"

"What? Eat? Make a living?"

"The schools are the key."

"Yeah, public schools are known for showering people with money."

Davis's phone beeps. It's Hattie. "I gotta take this."

"What the hell, man?"

"I'll call you back. I promise." Davis taps his phone, switching over to his wife. "Hi."

"I don't want to fight."

Davis grips the phone, allowing a smile. He takes another sip of whiskey letting it burn the good burn. He doesn't want to fight either. After all these years. After all the recent arguments over money, over everything, simply hearing her voice can still bring a smile. A sudden feeling of calm.

"Good. I'd rather not do that either," he says. "I'm sorry. I don't do travel very well. I really am tired."

"You sound like it. Where are you, at a bullfight?"

"No," he says, covering, not wanting to get into a discussion about his *edges*. "I'm meeting some potential clients at a bar. Not my thing, but ya know."

"Fancy. It'll be better when you come home," Hattie says over the sound of the girls laughing and playing in the background. "You've got some clients here who would love to talk with you. Will you take the meeting, Mr. Briggs?"

He smiles even wider, pressing the phone closer to his ear. "I accept."

The conversation is a short, jumbled mess of high-pitched *I love yous* and semi-coherent stories about school and recess tragedies, but it's what Davis needed. His shoulders relax again. His mood softens as the raging storm of nouns, verbs and adjectives from the mouths of his daughters pours over him.

In a flash he remembers when they were born.

That trip to the beach.

Watching movies on Friday nights. A highlight reel of the good.

Then his brain, as it always does, transitions to worry. To the things that cost. To the things that cost money they do not have.

The business is failing.

He is failing.

His family.

Everyone.

His concentration slips over to the girls growing up. Costs of braces. Dance lessons. First cars. Clothes. College. He lets his eyes shift out of focus as he takes another drink. The whiskey slides down his throat, his vision a blur of color and light.

He hears the phone being fumbled back over to his wife.

"Well," Hattie says, "I need to wrestle these two into bed and get some work done before tomorrow."

Davis snaps out of his trance. "Good luck," he says.

"You sure you're okay? Do you need to talk about anything?"

That's the last thing Davis wants to do.

Talk. Talk about anything.

"I'm fine," he says. "I'll get some sleep and crush it tomorrow."

Even as the words leave his lips he knows that's complete bullshit. He shakes it off then says goodnight to his wife, ending the conversation with a half-hearted *I love you.*

He drains the drink, then motions to the bartender for another. He needs to let his mind dull, to stop it from churning things over and over again. Stop the spin cycle of worry. He starts thumbing through social media on his phone, looking for a distraction.

Wishes he hadn't.

There are pics of Todd living the life of Todd. Pics at parties. Todd with various women. Drinks, smiles and tanned, toned bodies everywhere. Todd's most recent skiing vacation. Vegas. His time learning to surf. His time hiking. His freedom. His family money backing him up so he can start a business with a friend.

Davis doesn't have a net. It's just him and Hattie.

He shakes his head with a smirk. "Son of a bitch."

His phone buzzes. Speaking of the son of a bitch. "Yes, Todd."

"Dude."

"Don't start. I'm exhausted. I'll go to the last pitch tomorrow morning, then I'll fly back. You can beat me up all you want when I get home."

"I don't want to beat you up, and for the record, I don't want to talk you into anything you don't want to do."

"That's exactly what you want to do."

"True, but that's what I do."

The beautiful woman Davis saw outside the hotel sits down next to him.

"You going to talk to me now, Shy One?" she asks, her voice coated in sugar. "This seat taken?"

Davis's eyes almost pop from his head. His pulse begins to dance. He fumbles around his tongue like a junior high kid talking to girl in the lunchroom.

"Who the hell is that?" Todd asks.

"No," Davis says as he hangs up on Todd, setting his phone on the bar. "All yours."

The woman takes the seat close to Davis while leveling him with those eyes, along with that same warm smile she laid on him earlier outside. She lets his semi-buzzed gaze get its fill, making sure he has time to get a full understanding of what is sitting next to him. This is a woman who could sit down anywhere, next to any man in this or any other bar, and she's chosen to sit next to Davis.

An idea shreds through his head like a runaway train.

The same idea any married man has had, at least once.

A fantasy.

He's never cheated on Hattie, never wanted to. He's thought about it, of course, but never felt the need to truly pursue it in any real kind of way. Harmless flirting here and there, but never anything vaguely serious.

This idea, fantasy, the one he's having right now, is probably simply the spawn of an idea sparked earlier by this same woman when he saw her outside. He knows this will go nowhere, but it's been a long time since he's talked to someone like this. Actually, if he's being honest with himself, he's never talked to anyone like this. This fantasy, however, has legs. It's growing roots. There's a specific feeling spreading.

This feeling is not about sex. It's not about reaching orgasm with another woman. As fun as that would be, this is not about that at all and Davis knows it.

This is about being wanted. Being wanted in *that* way. Being desired by an attractive woman and the high that can come along with it. Call it ego or self-esteem masturbation, Davis doesn't care about the label. Right now, he cares about feeling that way again and wants to make it last as long as possible.

A feeling that has been lost. Shoved in a drawer and long forgotten.

The way Davis felt in high school when that cheerleader said *hi*, winked and later made out with him in the woods at that keg party that one summer. It was how he felt when he bought that girl from his English class two Mind Erasers at that shitty piano bar in college.

What was the name of that joint?

That dude always played "Piano Man" and "American Pie" while the drunks wailed off-key. He couldn't tell you a damn thing about any class he took in college, but he can tell you everything about that night. They talked for hours about music and movies, then later had clumsy sex in his cramped dorm room.

Hell, what was her name?

Did they have sex or did Davis just imagine it later?

The years fog a man's mind on many subjects, usually filling in the blank spots with the most flattering details they can think of, often shading the truth slightly with a filter that helps them push through life with their head held high.

Sexual success is not immune to a man's mental refresh.

The answers don't find their way to the front of Davis's wandering, half-buzzed mind, but that feeling is clear. That one coming up in full color, high resolution, surround sound as if it had happened only yesterday.

Davis's eyes scan over the polished, jaw-dropping twentysomething seated next to him. She's looking at him with wild, searing blue eyes and a brutal, unique beauty that has turned heads probably all her life.

"Tilley," she says, extending a hand.

Davis blinks, looking at her hand, but quickly realizes it's his turn.

"I'm Davis. Drink?" He shakes her hand, fighting to find some cool.

Tilley looks him up and down. "You're married." She says it not as a question but more as an accusation.

"Yes, sorry. Drink?"

"Vodka tonic. Lime. Don't be sorry. Kids?"

Davis gets the bartender's attention. "Vodka tonic with lime for her, for Tilley." He turns back to her. "Yes. Yeah, I have kids. Two girls."

Tilley lights up. Warmth washes over her face. Her eyes flicker as she says, "I love kids. You're a good man. I'm pretty good at judging people."

"Thank you."

She nods then returns to her normal, steady state of blistering sexuality. "But you are sitting here. Did you wander in here looking for me?"

"Wanted a drink before calling it a day," Davis says, shifting his seat, struggling to look relaxed in front of her. Trying to act as if he does this all the time.

He does not.

Tilley takes a long pull off her vodka. The ice clinks against the glass. She throws him a look. "It's okay to admit it. The marriage thing." She leans in. "Doubt anybody here is going to tell on you." She lowers head and whispers, "Not here."

Davis lets out a nervous chuckle.

If he heard how awkward it sounded, he'd crawl under the bar.

Tilley lets him off the hook, leans back and clinks her glass with his.

She lets a tense, yet flirty, beat of time pass, then leans toward him again. This time into his ear, letting her words dance off her tongue. "It's five hundred for the first thirty minutes. I do just about everything, all with mind-melting skill."

Davis almost spits out his drink again, a near-perfect spit take this time.

Tilley smiles big, as does the bartender.

"You are a mess. Look at you," she says. "All you're doing is having a drink."

"Really, is that all that's happening?"

She fires him a gaze that would peel the pants off a dead man and readies herself for the kill shot as she cocks her head with a slight grin. Tucking a strain of hair behind her ear she says, "We're strangers, right?"

"I guess so."

"There's freedom in that, right?" Tilley wets her lips. "What if we showed each other our dark sides, our strange sides, did all the things you wouldn't dare do with someone else. All this could be a simple, wonderful, cherished memory between"—she touches her finger to his chest then hers—"you and I."

Davis feels his insides shake. His hands twitch and itch. He has no idea what expression he has on his face, but it can't be cool. No idea what the correct way to respond is. This is all new for Davis. Exciting and uncomfortable at the same time.

She is stunning.

In a flash of a second, he makes some calculations on how much cash he can get, but quickly dismisses the idea. He's not that guy. He hates that he's not, but he knows he's not. Todd would have already had sex with her, paid her and be sound asleep by now.

She sits. Waiting for an answer. A sign of life from Davis. She holds his eyes, smacks her lips with pop. "Well?"

Davis drains his drink, closes his eyes and says, "I can't." He wants to pick the words out of the air and throw them away, but deep down he knows it was the right thing to say.

Tilley smiles.

"I'd love to," he tells her, keeping his eyes shut. "You're very nice, gorgeous and unbelievable and... I can't. I'm sorry."

"Don't be sorry, handsome." She touches his hand then kisses him softly on the cheek. "You're a good boy. Nothing to be ashamed of."

She slinks off, disappearing into the crowd with heads turning as she passes.

Davis finally opens his eyes.

He takes in a deep, deep breath and orders up another drink. Deep regret mixed with the opposing feeling of knowing he did the right thing wages a tiny war inside of him. Punching holes through every molecule of his being. Yes, he did do the right thing, he knows it, but damn it sucks.

Never in a million years did he think he'd be in that situation. Propositioned by a prostitute. A hooker in a fancy LA hotel bar. A scene right out of a movie. It'll make a great story to tell Todd when he gets back. One day, he'll tell Hattie too. She'll think it's funny, if he tells it right. He snickers to himself just thinking of the idea that he'd even considered having sex with a *lady of the night*. Not something Davis Briggs would do.

"You are a better man than me."

Davis turns to find someone new has taken the seat next to him.

4

SITTING NEXT to him now is a man.

A slick man dressed in a suit Davis could only hope to afford. A man lifted from a Hollywood set. The same good-looking man he saw walking with Tilley outside the hotel.

"Justin Reed." He shakes Davis's hand, flashing a pirate smile.

"Davis."

"Davis, you are one strong-willed bastard."

"What? Why?"

"You turned that woman down. You did see her, right? Your eyes work properly, not blind or some shit?" Justin laughs as he snags a cherry from the bar. "Fairly sure that's never happened to her, ever. Not sure she's ever heard the word *no* about anything. Hell, she's probably flipped a few gay guys to the other side. What I'm saying is what you just did takes some kinda strength, brutha. Kind I've only read about. Heard songs about. Mythical, industrial-grade shit."

"Weren't you two together outside?"

"Something like that." Justin motions to the bartender. "Let's get a bottle of what he's having." He snaps his fingers then points toward Davis. "You in? Hack it up between us?"

The bartender clears his throat, looking dead at Davis, remembering his previous spit take about the price of a single glass. "It's three hundred a bottle."

Davis wants to scream out *NO*.

No way he can do this.

Hattie will kill him.

He can maybe get away with the hotel bill, but he knows damn well that he'd have to do a financial juggling act with that kind of bar tab. The hotel alone is going to rub up against the max of one card. Maybe could use another credit card for the bar. One that's close to maxing out too, teetering on getting declined, but with some wiggle room around the edges.

The pride burning inside will not let him walk away. Something in Davis will not allow him to admit he can't afford it. To tell Justin, or himself, that he's not there yet.

Fake it until you make it.

"Yeah, why not." Davis pulls a card and lays it

down next to Justin's. He can only hope he pulled the right one.

Davis can't help but notice even Justin's credit card is better than his. Justin's is sleek, black and shines as if it were polished. Looks as if it's made of military-grade, bulletproof material. Probably has a six-figure credit limit.

Davis's card is tied to a local wholesale club.

He gets points.

There's a hum of electricity to Justin. A bolt of life to everything he does. The way he drinks his drink. There's a certain style to how he holds his glass, to how he sips his whiskey. It's as if everything he does has been figured out ahead of time. Preplanned, rehearsed cool. Davis remembers reading that Steve McQueen practiced opening and closing a car door over and over again while filming *Bullitt* so he could find the way that looked the coolest on film.

Justin was born knowing the coolest way to do things.

Davis thinks he's spent his life perusing the opposite. A life spent tracking down the most uncool way of doing everything.

"I love whiskey," Justin says. "Hate LA, but love whiskey."

Davis laughs and nods. "Yeah, I can understand that. What do you do, Justin?"

"Do?"

"Yeah, do for a living."

"It's funny. I spent a month in Australia on business last year and let me tell you, man, those folks got shit figured the hell out."

The bartender cracks open the bottle, serving two fresh glasses.

Justin gives a thumbs-up while continuing. "Work is something they do for money. That's it. Their job doesn't define them, just a thing they do so they can have food and shelter. They let their life define them. Not work." Justin pauses, shakes his head in disbelief. "Here it not only defines us, it's how we introduce ourselves."

"Sounds nice."

"Sorry, you were just being polite and I'm being a complete douche. But to answer your question"—Justin clinks glasses with Davis—"I make sure people have a good time."

Davis scrunches his nose. "A good time?"

"A great time, actually."

"What does that mean?"

"People hire me to show people the time of their lives."

Davis takes a sip, trying to digest that statement.

Justin smiles, as if this is the response he gets all the time.

"Sometimes it's a casino courting a whale," Justin explains. "Maybe a Hollywood studio wants to sign talent. More than once a CEO of a large corporation has used my services as a gift, or a gift for themselves. And as many athletes and celebrities can attest, discretion is my natural state."

Justin never breaks eye contact with Davis as he explains. Each word is chosen, polished and served to his new friend on a silver platter. He offers no apology for what he's saying, nor does he have a hint of shame. He doesn't come across as boasting either.

He is merely stating facts.

Davis is mesmerized. This is a peek into a world that he is not familiar with.

"Trust is the main thing. You spend a lifetime building it and can lose it in the blink of an eye. If you remove the trust between people, there's nothing to hold on to. Don't you agree?"

Davis nods, not completely sure what he's agreeing to. He doesn't have these types of conversations at the swim meets. At dance lesson drop-offs. Nobody talks like this at the cookouts or those damn PTA meetings. This guy Justin has a magic to him. Has the world by the balls and doesn't even seem to care about the grip he's using. Seems almost bored with it.

This is the first time in forever Davis can remember having an interesting conversation with anyone. An actual verbal exchange with an interesting person. They are not discussing lawn care, schools or the best way to get to work. There's no talk about what needs to be fixed at the house, or bought, or money issues, or a problem that needs to be solved, or something he isn't doing correctly.

Davis finds himself wanting to keep this going, if only for a moment. He knows he can't afford another drop from this bottle, but he can't stop. Not now.

"So that woman, the one who was just here, she does what?" Davis takes a drink then lowers his voice. "She works with you?"

Justin smiles, winks, takes a drink as well, and shrugs his shoulders. "So, Davis, what do you do?"

"Me?"

"Yeah."

"My work doesn't define me, Justin," Davis says with a laugh.

"I apologize." Justin laughs, putting a hand on Davis's shoulder as if they've been friends forever. "Strike the question."

"Okay, fine," Davis says, starting to feel the whiskey. "I'm here pitching my new company."

"Oh, that sounds cool."

"It is. We've started a software company that's about to blow up huge."

"Yeah?"

"It's going to solve a big problem."

"Problem?"

"Yeah, a problem with how we communicate."

"Sounds heavy, man."

Davis snickers, the whiskey well past doing its job.

Justin refills their glasses. "A lot of money in tech," Justin says. "Metric shit ton of money, if I may be so bold. You gotta be doing well, right?"

Davis looks into his glass, letting his understanding of the truth flicker then fade into the background. He lets that truth dissipate out into the air, floating away like smoke drifting out into the noise of the crowd mixing in with the thumping bass. He allows the fact that the walls are caving in to slip away from his mind. The fact that his company, his dream, his everything is currently on the ropes? Davis lets those lumps of unpleasant truth to simply melt.

The debt.

The failure to land clients.

The arguments with family and friends. Hattie. Todd.

He wants to press pause on all of it, if only for the moment, to let the facts drift away. To take a vacation from himself.

It feels good. Nice. Great even. Letting go is freedom. Denial, his private Fiji.

"Yeah," Davis says, slugging back more whiskey, "it's going really well."

"Cool." Justin clinks his glass again. "Good on

you, man. Getting anything done in this shit world is worthy of a goddamn parade."

Davis wishes any word of that sentence—*it's going really well*—were true.

"Glad I met you, Davis." Justin runs his tongue over his teeth, raises his eyebrows and stares toward Davis like he wants to say something.

"What?" Davis asks.

Tilley slinks over behind him.

She doesn't say a word. She doesn't have to. She puts an arm around Davis and gives that damn smile. Davis smiles back. The whiskey and the conversation are melting that mythical strength Justin was complimenting him on only moments ago.

"Well, sir," Justin says, "this is where I need to ask you a really important question."

Davis fights to hold on to that small part of him that's in control. The part that knows the value of the word *No*. He looks between the two of them then puts his hands up as if calling for mercy.

"Look, guys," he says, "I appreciate this but—"

"Don't you want to hear the question?" Justin asks.

"Guys—"

"You should at least hear the question," Tilley says.

Davis takes in a deep breath, letting the excitement dig its claws into him while his head buzzes.

The feeling off the whiskey has hit him fast and hard. Harder than he's ever experienced. It's a sharper buzz than he's used to. Feels different than drunk. He blinks his eyes, working to find some focus.

"I think, this is just me now, but I do think"—Tilley leans in close, letting her blue eyes hypnotize—"you should hear what the man has to say."

Davis nods, powerless to respond otherwise.

"Good." Justin takes a drink, then leans in too. "Would you like to see what I do for yourself?"

Tilley squeezes Davis's arm. Davis feels his heartbeat accelerate even faster.

"What?" Davis asks, clearing his throat, his head hitting a full-on drunk.

"Sorry." Justin shakes his head. "I wasn't being clear." He glances to Tilley, then lets his eyes slip back over to Davis. "You ready for the time of your life?"

PART II

5

———

Davis forces his eyelids open.

His head is on fire. Pounding like a drum. His vision a soup-like fog, with blobs of smeared colors cut up by shafts of light.

As he sits up, his stomach turns. Quickly he realizes he did this way too fast. There's a rush of nausea coupled with a whirling whip-spin inside his head. He's been hungover before, but this is different. This cuts like a knife, but is dull at the same time. His fuzzy memory fights to find clarity. Not much there to cling to, however there are some things that are as clear as can be.

As his head and sight come back online he remembers jagged pieces of last night.

He remembers talking with Todd.

With Hattie. With the girls.

Looking around the room, something seems off

to him. It looks like his room. Seems familiar. The colors of the walls, the décor are all the same, but the room feels different. Davis smacks his lips, moving his tongue around the inside of his mouth, hoping to find some form of moisture.

It's not there. It's a mouthful of cotton-wrapped sandpaper.

On the bedside table is a tall glass of water with an iceberg mass floating at the top. Next to it are four Ibuprofen, what looks like an antacid pill and some eye drops. All laid out neatly in separate rows on a black napkin. Looks like it's made of silk. A thoughtful care package set out with deliberation.

Did I do that?

How is the ice not melted?

He doesn't remember getting ice last night, doesn't remember getting himself a glass of water this morning, and he certainly doesn't remember laying out pills and hangover supplies for himself on a satin napkin. He doesn't even know where he would have gotten one. His phone is on the charger lying next to him on bed.

Looking down, he's dressed in a pair of boxers he doesn't recognize. They're silk as well. Black too. They seem new. Not something he owns.

Looking around the room, everything is in order. Everything in its right place. His suitcase is open, but all of his clothes are folded neatly inside. Even what he had on last night. Davis wouldn't know the first thing about packing a bag like that. When he leaves a hotel he wads everything up into his suitcase and jams it closed best he can, often testing the engineering of the zipper. His black workbag is zipped up, sitting next to the suitcase.

He remembers Justin.

What happened?

He remembers Tilley.

I turned them down. Didn't I? Oh God, what happened?

Davis jumps up from the bed, ignoring the storm raging in his head. Compartmentalizes the sudden drop in his stomach and the aches in his bones. There's no sign of someone else being there or having been there. No shoes. No empty bottles or dirty glasses. No women's clothes. No scent of perfume. Nothing.

He rushes to the bathroom.

Not the way I left it.

Toothbrush. Toothpaste. Shaving gear. It's all laid out carefully, in perfectly spaced rows on the now familiar black satin napkins. The towels are all folded perfectly and stacked in their proper place. There's not even a drop of water anywhere in the sink or on the counter.

"What the hell?" Davis mutters, checking himself in the mirror.

His hair is neatly combed. Perfect. His face is clean-shaven. He feels his skin. His hands, his arms, his body are soft with lotion. His fingernails and toenails have been attended to and cared for as well.

Stepping out from the bathroom he sees the clock. It reads twelve noon. Davis hasn't slept past six a.m. in years.

Fragments of last night are crawling back to him now. Pulses of memory pop up in bursts and flashes. He remembers talking on the phone outside the hotel. Meeting Tilley at the bar, then Justin. Justin talking about his business.

What he does for a living.

Australia.

Talking about trust.

He remembers coming back to the room before he went to the bar, slamming his fist into the wall and knocking down the picture. Turning toward the wall, Davis's heart skips a row of beats. There's a picture hanging on the wall, but there's no broken glass. The glass is perfect. It's not the same picture. It's a black and white picture of a beautiful beach, not the crashing wave photo.

Davis spins around, his eyes dancing, scanning the rest of the room. He sees it now. This is different. The bed is on the wall on the other side of the room. The chairs are in a different corner. He throws open the curtains. It's overlooking the pool, not the view of the front of the hotel from last night where he watched the cars come and go.

This isn't my room.

Panic fires through Davis. He dives toward the bed, grabbing his phone. There are a ton of missed calls and texts. For a flash of second he feels hopeful; maybe it's people from the meetings he took. Maybe they are placing orders. It's not.

There are several from Todd. Davis skips those.

There's a single text from Justin.

Great time, man. You really needed that. We'll settle up later.

What the hell? When did he get my number? Settle what?

Most of texts are from Hattie.

Any better today?

Did you really need to call at 3AM?

Are you okay?

Where are you?

Did you miss your flight? Davis steps back, his mind flipping. *Miss my flight?* Confusion spiking, he checks the date of the last text. He lets the phone drop to the bed.

He's missed an entire day.

6

Davis grabs the phone from the bed.

He doesn't know what he's going to say, but he has to tell Hattie something.

Something that will give him some time to think.

Time for him to figure out what the hell is going on.

His brain scrambles. His emotions redline.

With hands shaking he dials HOME.

"Davis?" Hattie picks up on a half ring. Her voice is panicked. Tired.

"I'm sorry."

"What happened? I was up all night. Are you okay?"

"I'm so, so sorry." Davis glances to his black bag, looking for something to say. Stable ground to build from. "I... I was out with a lead at the bar last night. A big one. They wanted to go out." He closes his eyes, hating how easily the lies on top of a lie are coming to him. "One drink turned into two and so on."

"You couldn't call or text?"

"They're old-school hard-asses. They wanted my full attention. They hate people using phones all the time. I lost track of time. Had way too much drink."

"Jesus, Davis. You know you're not a big drinker."

"I know. I shouldn't have tried to keep up with them, but I wanted the business. It got out of control, then they brought me back to the hotel and I passed out. I just woke up."

"Oh baby, how do you feel?"

"Like complete shit." *For more reasons than one.* "I hope I didn't screw it all up."

"It'll be okay," Hattie says, coming down. Her tone has softened, replaced with genuine concern. "When are you leaving?"

"I'm heading to LAX in a minute to figure out a flight back."

"Okay. I'm... I'm just glad you're okay. I was worried. I didn't know what to tell the girls."

"I know. I'm sorry."

"Just come home. I've got to go into the office, but I should be back before you land."

Davis almost hangs up.

"I love you," Hattie says.

Her words cut his heart in half. He doesn't know what happened in LA. He knows he turned Justin and Tilley's offer down, at least he thinks he did, but the idea that something could have happened is killing him.

Did I? Did I actually do something wrong? Why can't I remember any of it?

His stomach twists. His head spins. It all happened so damn fast. There's so much he doesn't know, and now, all the lies he's told.

"I love you too."

He hangs up.

He wants to break down, wants to release the emotions swelling inside of him, but he gets ahold of himself. He wants to throw his guts up, actually, but controls his insides as they weave into a pretzel.

Davis slumps down to the bed, giving his shaking knees some sort of relief. He turns toward the front of the room. There's something he didn't notice before. Squinting, he sees what looks like a greeting card standing up on the dresser next to the TV. Davis stands up, taking a closer look at the card. It's a glossy, stark white card with elegant black script that simply reads, DAVIS BRIGGS.

He opens the card.

He wants to drop through the floor.

To escape.

The inside of the card asks...
DID YOU HAVE THE TIME OF YOUR LIFE?

7

Davis's head throbs hard as the cab pulls away from the Viceroy.

The world is still in a fog. There's still a thick haze coating his senses, but it's better than before. At least he can make things out better. Objects are more than blobs. He doesn't have to expend so much energy to focus on understanding words and images.

Hopefully he can get on standby for a flight home. He just hung up with the airline and there's a decent chance he can get on at least one flight today. There are three more if he misses this one that seem to have greater than zero odds, but the last one leaves at ten p.m. Fighting security at LAX isn't going to be fun given his physical state, but he'll gut it out.

What choice does he have? He needs to get home. This needs to end.

Davis hates this feeling, even though he's not completely sure what *this* is. Guilt is taking hold of him even though he doesn't know that he has anything to truly feel guilty about. He doesn't remember doing anything wrong, but obviously something happened.

That room. What the hell was with that room?

His belongings were all tended to. Tended to better than even he would have done. He was dressed in boxers he did not own. Davis fumbles through where he went wrong. What mistake did he make? Yes, he shouldn't have gone down to the bar. Yes, he probably shouldn't have even engaged in conversation with Tilley, but hell man.

He was only talking to her.

How can I not remember more? Was I drugged?

He doesn't remember taking anything. Doesn't remember seeing them slip him anything. There was no evidence of it in the room and, more importantly, why would they drug him? They didn't steal anything from the room. All his credit cards are there, not that there was any available credit on any of them, and the cash he brought is still in his wallet.

What was their game? What's in it for them?

He remembers emotions more than actual events. Flares of feelings, not images of the night that's passed him by. Thoughts slip and fumble around, all struggling to find some form of stable ground. He's becoming more and more frustrated that he can't piece together anything that happened.

He remembers feeling listened to. Feeling wanted.

Not a normal thing. Todd never listens to him. That'd be a first. Hattie rarely does. The girls only do because they're still too young for rebellion, but that's right around the corner. He knows it. He's heard from friends and neighbors all the horror stories about raising girls.

None of those feelings of being ignored are new.

They've been coming on for a while. He's felt it building up more and more recently. The growing tension in his marriage. All the ties of his life gripping tight around him, cutting into him. Middle age and so on. Could be that maybe last night was the blowup. The middle-aged crazy story he's heard jokes about all these years. Was last night the perfect storm of being out of town, drinking and the chance meeting of the wrong, beautiful people?

Did I get drunk and take it too far?

Davis wraps his head in his hands as if trying to rub hard enough to bring the memories back to life. Cerebral CPR. It's not working. Whatever knocked him out, be it booze or drugs, it did its job and did it well. Covered its tracks and cleared the evidence without a smudge of a fingerprint. He strains and shuts his eyes tight, stretching out to the farthest corners of his failing memory, but he can see nothing past Justin and Tilley at the bar.

Their smiles. Their eyes looking back at him, welcoming him into their world. A world that looked inviting as hell.

The cab stops at LAX. The busy international airport is a whirlwind of chaos. Cars, SUVs, buses and cabs scream in and out. Hard stops. Fast starts. Quick jerks of steering wheels. Horns blare. Loved ones give rushed kisses. Others scream obscenities out cracked windows. Davis gets dizzy simply watching the world rip and roll around him.

"Fifty-two thirty-five," the cab driver says without looking his way.

Davis has no clue if that's accurate or if he's getting screwed, but he pulls his Visa out anyway. He takes a deep breath before the slide. He hasn't been this nervous about a credit card transaction in long time. Like playing a slot machine of sorts. Hoping for a good outcome. The cab's credit card terminal pauses, blinks, then...

DECLINED.

In a snap of an instant Davis's world crashes down even harder.

It's been years since he's had a card declined. Been years since they ran up the debt to that point.

They spent years paying it off. A long, hard climb that almost ended his marriage. Hattie said she never wanted to feel that way again. He convinced her it was different this time. With this business, he could make it work. They were smarter this time.

She loves him, trusts him.

She held his hand on this leap of faith.

He tries the card again.

Same.

"What..." Davis is finding it hard to breath. He slaps a heavy palm on the terminal. "What the hell, man?"

"Easy, boss. It's been acting up," the cab driver says, turning back toward him now. "Do you have another card? Cash still works, bro."

Davis pulls out his wallet. All he has is the company card and some cash. He really doesn't want to use the company card, which is getting real damn close to hitting the redline max too. Getting declined twice in thirty seconds might be too much to take. Counting out his cash, plus tip, it'll clean him out, but what choice does he have?

He hands it over to the driver and jumps from the cab. Time is running out.

Racing to the security line, he pulls up his e-ticket on his phone and gets his driver's license ready. His phone buzzes in his hand. He's got a new text burning a red number one.

A text from Justin.

When u leaving, big fun?

Davis thinks of replying. He has no idea what to say, but he wants so bad to know what the hell happened. How do you even start with something like this? How do you phrase the question, assuming Justin will even tell him anything? Davis's fingers hover over this phone. He doesn't have the words as his fingertips shake just above the glass. Truth is, he's not sure he wants answers to the questions he can't bring himself to ask.

What was I thinking? Did I ruin everything?

Justin Reed is trouble. A problem that needs to go away. Davis will change his number if he has to, but he can't engage with this guy. He needs to let this die and come to an end on its own. A guy like Justin will get bored and leave him alone eventually.

He ignores the text.

Davis swipes over to the ticket on his phone then rushes toward the security line with his driver's license ready in his other hand.

Time to go.

Just come home, Hattie said.

8

———

Davis walks into his house.

There's a tingle in his fingers. A flutter in his stomach.

His girls rush to his knees, squeezing tight with all they've got. He's only been gone a day or so, but they're young enough to not know the difference. All they know is daddy was not here and they didn't care for it, no matter how long. He forgets his thoughts about their upcoming college costs. Their braces. Their weddings. Their pending rebellion against him. They love him now, even though they forget sometimes, and that's enough. He lets the warmth that comes from their little arms wash over his body. His eyes well as he touches the soft hair on their tiny, wonderful heads.

"Hi," Hattie says.

Davis looks up, sees his beautiful wife walking

into the room. She remarkably looks the same as the day they met in college when they locked eyes as their fingers fumbled over a keg all those years ago. Those two buzzed, slightly horny kids never would have imagined they'd be standing here almost twenty years later.

Married. A house. Two kids.

Kinda crazy when you think about it in those terms.

She's still dressed from work, but has on her feet the ridiculous black and white cow slippers he got her for Christmas. Davis smirks, acknowledging the fashion choice. Hattie shrugs.

"Hungry?" she asks, maneuvering through the girls and stealing a kiss.

Davis nods. "I'm sorry," he says.

She nods her head along with an understanding look. "Did the client get disgusted by your lack of tolerance?"

She's teasing, but Davis can read between the lines.

He holds her eyes, lost in his thoughts.

He thinks about telling her everything, wanting to lay the truth out for her right here, right now. They've been through so much together. Things much harder than this LA trip. At least as far as he can remember about the LA trip. He thinks of the incredible release that would come from unloading this burden he's been carrying around since this morning. The lies he's told her to cover up a truth he's not even sure of. It would be a difficult conversation, to be sure, but she'd understand. He's sure she would. There might be a fight, but it'd be over soon. They could put it in their rearview mirror and that would be that. He didn't do anything, after all.

Did I?

"I've got to get some work done after dinner," she says, "but you'll tell me all about it later?"

Davis blinks. "What?"

"Your trip. The accounts, all that," she says. "I want to hear this story."

Davis swallows then nods.

There have been many times Davis has marveled at how she manages to do it all. She's a successful marketing manager for a major clothing store, yoga queen and a super mom candidate if ever there was one. Juggling it all as if it wasn't even there. As if this was something she's done her whole life. There's no online training for what she does. No bonus payout for being everything for your family.

"The client is okay, right?" Hattie asks.

She wants more out of life. She'd never say it, but he knows it. She has to. A woman like her wants more, right? She doesn't want to scrape by, living redline to redline.

Davis doesn't have the heart to tell her

anything other than, "I'll know more soon, but I hope my lack of drinking skill didn't ruin everything."

It's like *didn't ruin everything* has been nailed to the wall of his brain. Did he subconsciously throw that out there?

She smirks and retreats back into the kitchen to finish up dinner.

It's a bomb waiting to detonate. He knows it. He comforts himself, knowing that at least he knows how to disarm it. He can tell her. Come clean. He'll tell her later, he tells himself. When the time is right.

"I'll do the dishes," he says.

She laughs from the kitchen. "Damn right, Hollywood."

The girls are still hanging from his legs. He Frankenstein-walks them into the living room, leaving his bags at the door. The dog now joins in on the attack, jumping up, fighting for a good lick. Davis falls down on the couch in a pile of children, daddy and dog. The girls giggle. The dog licks. The daddy smiles.

He's home. With his people.

There's a sting of knowing how close he came to screwing this all up. He feels a lump in his throat. He can't believe where his head was not long ago. That he allowed the stress of the business, the lure of booze and the excitement of sexy people to take hold of him that way. That he allowed it all to take him close to a place that would jeopardize this.

He tickles the girls with reckless abandon and pets the dog while dodging a massive slurping tongue.

His phone buzzes.

A shot of anxiety rips through him. He stands straight up, reaching for his phone.

"Dad-dy," the girls say in unison.

He checks the text.

It's Justin.

Duuuuude…. Where r u?

"Dad-dy."

Davis's mood shifts in a snap. His face hardens as he stares into the screen of his phone. Almost looking through it. As if the house and family around him have been cropped from his senses.

He feels his stomach flutter then drop again as it did in his hotel room in LA.

He grinds his teeth.

He can't even hear his girls anymore.

9

———

THE MORNING SUN cuts through the blinds, creating shafts of light across the bedroom like bars from an Old West jailhouse.

Davis is rolled over on his side staring at his phone. He can hear Hattie waging an all-out war with the girls down the hall. The daily give and take, all in the name of getting them to school. He slept some, but not well. Lots of turning, broken, scattered rest, but calling it *sleep* is a stretch.

Davis is staring at a new text from Justin that came in at 2 a.m.

r u ignoring me?

2:36 a.m.

need to talk soon, bro

3:07 a.m.

hello you owe

Davis rolls his eyes. Annoyed this isn't going away as quickly as he wanted.

Justin isn't getting bored as Davis had hoped.

Davis has had some time to think about it. Some time to sleep on it, so to speak, even if he didn't truly sleep much. He knows he should just contact this guy, get it over with, have the damn conversation that he'd rather not have. Tell this guy to go to hell and leave him alone. Still, he's willing to give it more time, let it play itself out. He hasn't been home a full twenty-four hours yet.

A few annoying texts?

Davis is more than happy to let this go a little longer.

Conflict is not something Davis seeks out, and this Justin situation more than qualifies as potential conflict. Davis is not afraid to step up when called upon—he's had to go toe to toe with people in the past—but it's not something he enjoys. Todd loves to mix it up. Enjoys the fight and will go the long way around to find one. Davis is the cooler of the two heads.

He sets down the phone, telling himself he'll call Justin after he talks to Todd later this morning. Davis wants to talk this through with Todd. He needs his personal sounding board, business partner and friend to hear him out. This needs a conversation. A good one.

They're meeting for coffee at their normal spot.

Their office, otherwise known as a coffee shop.

He's been telling Todd, *We'll talk about it when I get back,* the whole time he was in LA and, well, now he is back. For better or worse. The business is another conflict chat Davis would rather not have, but unlike Justin, Davis can't avoid Todd.

"Shit," Davis grunts.

"Dad-dy," echoes from the hall.

"Shit," Davis grunts again as he drags himself from the bed.

As he sits up, an image of Tilley races across his brain.

This is new.

The mental picture stabs into his mind's eye like an icepick. It's not a memory from the bar. It was only for a fraction of a second, but there's no mistaking it was of her. She was on her back on the floor, staring up at him. He recognized the carpet. The pattern was from his room at the hotel. Her eyes were warm, inviting and she was smiling at him.

He shakes his head, rubs his face, and sits back down on the bed.

The image is gone now, leaving as quickly as it came.

He closes his eyes, straining to remember. Fighting for recall. He can't pull it back up. Can't access her face, a face he saw so clearly only a few seconds ago. His breath accelerates as he realizes he just had a memory, one he didn't have yesterday. Not much of one, more like a single flicker-frame of a memory, but one that has created a hell of a lot more questions than answers.

"Shit," he says. This time he can hear the fear in his own voice.

"Dad-dy."

"Davis," Hattie calls out. "Little help from the father?"

He shakes off the memory of Tilley's face. "Coming."

10

———

At the coffee shop, as expected, Todd isn't happy.

Not at all.

"What the hell, man?" he asks.

"I know." Davis sips his first coffee of the day, letting his eyes slip over toward the window. He watches the good people of Beaverton, Oregon go about their day. Smiling. Laughing. He wishes he were one of them. Davis has just explained how the meetings went and Todd's reaction is exactly what Davis has been dreading since he was pacing in front of the Viceroy. Precisely what he's been putting on hold until now.

"What..." Todd is frustrated as hell, but sucks in a deep breath, trying to hold it together. "What are we going to do?"

"I told you, I'm not a salesman."

"We don't need you to be the greatest salesman in the history of American salesmen. We need you to present the damn product. A product you designed. A product you love."

"I know."

"All you gotta do is talk. Talk about the damn thing the way you talk to me about it. The way you talk to Hattie about it. That will sell it, man. Your passion for the thing is goddamn inspiring. It inspired me for Christ's sake, and I'm incapable of being inspired."

Davis sips his coffee, letting the silence fill the space between them. Buying some time for Todd to come down a bit. Davis remembers Todd once telling him the greatest sales trick ever is getting the other guy to believe that what he's buying is *his* idea. The *salesman's dream* he called it. It took a long time for Davis to even understand the concept, let alone try to get it to work in the world. It's a trick that Todd can do, but Davis knows he cannot.

"I can try," Davis finally says.

"Damn right you can. You need to get out there and earn, or there will be no company. No product for you to love."

"Come on."

"You've seen the numbers, right?"

Davis nods. "I know."

"Yeah?" Todd says. "They are not good."

"I'll make this right."

"We better figure it the hell out or we are completely fucked, friend-o." Todd resets. "You're the creative. I'm the business guy. I understand. We've said it from the beginning and accepted it, but we're not big enough to completely separate roles. We've got to do a little of both."

"I know."

"Stop saying that. I know you *know*," Todd says with a hard edge.

Davis looks away, jamming his tongue into his cheek. He's holding back, and Todd can see it. He knows when he's gone too far with Davis.

"Shit. Sorry, man." Todd looks Davis over. "You okay? You look like you're not great. LA beat your ass?"

You have no idea, thinks Davis.

Davis considers telling Todd about Justin and everything about that night, but he doesn't. Not the right time. He's the right person, but he's not in the right frame of mind.

"I'm fine," Davis says. "Long trip. Just tired."

Todd taps his coffee cup. Nods. Checks out an attractive woman at the counter. "I can still make that call. They called me again, ya know."

"Todd. I—"

"I know you don't want to go that way, but damn, man."

"We could sell direct. Direct to customer. Online."

"Been over it a thousand times, cut it up a thousand different ways. Too expensive and we simply ain't got it."

"We can figure it out."

"Really? You want to take on mastering a new skill set on top of everything else?"

Davis sucks in a deep breath. He feels the walls caving in on him, again. The same old feelings of failure creeping in. Feelings of knowing you're good enough to get to a certain point, of getting close to success, touching the outer edges of it, but ultimately not being able to get there. Davis knows them well. As if he's standing at the ropes of an exclusive club watching seemingly everyone else get in, but not being allowed inside himself. The crushing thoughts of letting everyone in his entire world down enter into his mind as well. They come into play slowly, but they're here now.

Numbers roll through his head. Red, negative numbers printed on insufficient funds notices. Credit card statements. Words like DECLINE. Calls from phone reps spitting out words like DISCONNECT and DELINQUENT. Words like NO and SORRY. Phrases from friends and family like AT LEAST YOU TRIED and YOU'RE TALENTED, YOU'LL GET 'EM NEXT TIME.

"I've got two meetings today," Todd says. "There's another one I can't get to. They have to meet today or they're out."

"I'll take it."

"You sure?"

"Yes."

"You look like shit."

"Appreciate it."

"It's true."

"I'll take the meeting."

"You sure, guy?"

"I'll do the fucking meeting, Todd," Davis says with way more bite than he intended.

"Well." Todd leans back. He smiles, impressed by the sudden fire in his partner. "Well okay then." He holds his fist out for a bump.

Davis gives it to him with zero life to the gesture.

11

———

Davis sits in the office lobby.

His black workbag rests on his knees, which are bouncing up and down with manic, nervous energy. He can't help but feel like a kid waiting to see the principal.

The guy at the desk said it would be a few minutes, that they were wrapping up another meeting and it shouldn't long. Said things were *a little crazy this morning.*

Yeah, no shit, thinks Davis.

His heart is racing. He hates this. Presenting. The selling of things. Makes him feel dirty. Like a used car salesman pushing shitty hunks of metal on innocent people. Davis just wants to make things and have them go out into the world. He just wants to do good things. And if they make a few bucks? Even better. Actually, he hopes they make more than a few bucks. He knows he is more idealist than capitalist, but he's also not naive about the need for money in this life. He knows the world needs both. The dreamers and money-minded are both essential to keeping the whole machine running.

"Davis?" asks an older man walking toward him. His hair is cut close to the skull, with hip glasses and casual yet high-priced jeans and untucked shirt.

"Yes." Davis gets up. As he does, his bag drops to the floor. He clumsily kicks it, then picks it up, trying to be cool about it.

He's not.

"You find the place okay?" the hip older man asks, shaking his hand.

"Yeah, no problem."

"Good. Good," says the hip older man as he shows Davis toward a glass-walled conference room just down the hall from the lobby.

Davis's phone buzzes. He checks it. It's a text from Justin.

hate being ignored. U owe me $$$.

Davis's heart pumps a little faster now.

As he looks up from the phone, he sees they've turned the corner, entering into the large confer-ence room. It's like a giant fish bowl, with not a single solid wall to provide an ounce of privacy from the rest of the office. Inside the room is a long table that seats five on each side. Each side is filled with men and women, each more intimidating than the other. It's a packed house.

The hip older man takes his seat at the end of the table, making the room count now eleven people staring back at Davis. Waiting to be impressed. Hoping to be blown away by Davis. This intimidating collection of women and men are looking at him, waiting to be dazzled by whatever he's about to say.

Davis fumbles the phone into his pocket. He wants to run away, to hide.

They keep staring at him, waiting. Wanting.

Davis sets his bag down, feeling sweat from his neck sliding down the middle of his back.

"Can I have some water, please?"

————

OUTSIDE THE BUILDING, Davis sits on the curb with his bag sitting next to him in the street.

He's sweating like a hog. At least they gave him another bottle of water before they politely told him they were pressed for time.

Things are a little crazy today.

He guzzles down the bottle while trying to find something positive to take away from the meeting he completely blew only minutes ago. Replays the meeting over and over again in his head looking for something to cling to. He sees it all so clearly. Every tortuous moment he spent in front of them. Their faces. Their half-hearted questions as they looked at their phones. Their complete disinterest. Davis beats himself up over and over again as the movie replays, reliving his failure in a constant loop.

His stomach twists. His shoulders inch up closer and closer to his ears.

His phone buzzes.

"No," he says softly.

It buzzes again. It's a call. Davis doesn't want to look. He waits for the call to go to voice mail. Knowing he can't let it go, he checks the call. He breathes a sigh of relief that it's not Justin at least. *Thank God.*

There are three missed calls from Todd however.

He knows I'm in a meeting. He set it up for Christ's sake.

Davis has to call Todd back. There's no avoiding this. No sugarcoating the disaster that just happened in that conference room. After his performance during the LA meetings, he needs to get in front of this one with Todd while he can.

He calls Todd.

"What the fuck, Davis?" Todd screams before Davis can get a word out.

"I know—"

"You charged how much to the company in LA?" Todd asks. "On the corporate card? You lost your damn mind?"

Davis almost drops the phone.

"There's one for a grand, another for eight hundred and another for... Jesus, man."

Davis thinks as fast as he can, spinning through the trip, the places he went and amounts. He purposely avoided using the company card as much as possible. He has no idea what those charges are for or where they came from, but he can guess who was involved.

Justin. Had to be Justin, but when?

Davis's head scrambles for a rational excuse to serve up to Todd, something to feed him in order get through this until he can figure out what's going on.

"My card was stolen," Davis spits out.

"Bullshit."

"No. You can call them—"

"Davis."

"You have to talk to them. They—"

"I already called them."

Davis feels himself fall away, fumbling over himself in the moment. It was the tone Todd used, the way he said it. Like Davis was a pathetic child who had no chance of lying his way out of anything.

Davis pauses. Resets.

"Todd, I noticed it was missing while I was in the cab to the airport. Not sure when I lost it, or when it was stolen." Davis keeps talking, creating the narrative on the fly, letting the lies pour down like rain. "I didn't need it to check out of the hotel. I used my personal card for that. I didn't use it at the bar. I was buying drinks for myself and put those on my personal card too. I couldn't find it when I wanted to pay for the cab. I called the card company while I was in the security line at LAX. They must have screwed up and not registered my call."

There's silence on Todd's end of the call. The silence of someone processing.

"Dude," Todd finally says. "You had a really bad trip to the coast, didn't you?"

Davis exhales. Unclenches his fists.

"Get some rest," Todd says. "I'm not going to ask about your meeting today."

"Don't."

"I already heard. So... yeah, let's just leave at that."

Davis can feel the frustration from the other end of the phone. He thinks about saying something about the meeting, something positive in the way of an excuse, but he decides he's lied enough to the man for one day.

He ends the call, but as he does he sees two new texts. Davis holds his breath.

The first one is from Chase Fraud Alert for his personal credit card.

Text YES if you authorized a charge for $5,000 to JRFUNINC.

The second text is from Hattie.

Do you know what JR FUN INC is?!?

12

"What the hell is all that?" Hattie asks.

Davis shuts the door, sets his bag down.

"Want to let me in on where five grand went to in LA? Five grand we both know we do not have?" she presses.

"My card was stolen," Davis says. "I've called the credit card company."

Hattie looks down. "What does the fun in JR FUN INC stand for?"

"Hattie—"

"No, really. Explain it to me."

"Again, my card was stolen. I have no clue what that even is."

Hattie takes a beat, regains her cool, and tries again. "Why didn't you tell me about any of this?"

"It was a miserable trip. I guess I didn't want to go through it all again."

"Why didn't you cancel the card when you found out it was stolen?"

"I did." Davis moves closer to her. "I just went through all of this with Todd too. The corporate card was taken too."

He's finding it easy to be convincing because every part of that last sentence is true. He's told this story once, so a glossy feeling of false truth is starting take hold. A half-lie is the same as a half-truth. Even as he convinces himself he's doing the right thing, there is a heaviness in his chest as he talks to her. His subconscious is working him over.

The guilt is mounting.

The lies are piling up high in a hurry.

Hattie looks into her husband's eyes. She's suspicious, he can tell, but her desire to believe him is so strong she pushes the suspicion aside. For the moment, at least. She nods.

"They're going to clear the five grand off the card?"

"Yes, they told me they would. Might take a couple of days though."

Davis makes a quick calculation in his head. He can use what's left of their savings to pay off the five thousand, but he'll have to make that up somehow. She'll be checking the card online, he knows, and it will show as a payment rather than a credit by the card company. That part he can figure out later. Right now, he's backed into a corner and he has to claw his way out any way he can.

Think.

The charges might be his. He can't prove they aren't, even though he doesn't remember making any of them. Doesn't mean he didn't authorize it all. He doesn't know.

Think.

The call with Justin is becoming more and more inevitable.

He looks into Hattie's eyes, hoping she'll find a way to let this go. At least long enough for him to try and make it right. He just needs some time. More time to work it all through.

"Okay," Hattie says, letting her shoulders relax. "I'm sorry. I lost it. I just saw the text and panicked. The amount? The money, you know? That stuff still freaks me the hell out."

Davis nods. He knows how their past financial problems still weigh heavily on her. They drag him down too from time to time, but she's always been the more responsible of the two of them. The smarter of the two, if he's being honest.

"I'm sorry too," he says.

She smiles, gliding closer to him. "What are you sorry for? You didn't do anything."

Davis swallows hard and forces a smile. "I should have told you about it. All of it."

"It's okay. Let's drop it." Hattie wraps her arms

around his neck. "The girls won't be home for a while."

"Yeah." His mind is swimming, not getting what she's saying at all.

"*Yeah?* That's all you've got?" Hattie grabs his face, forcing his full attention, and repeats her words for clarity's sake. "The girls won't be home for a while."

"Oh."

"Yeah, *oh.*"

She kisses him softly. It takes him a second to let go of all that's happened, but he returns the kiss, allowing it all to melt away for the time being.

"You okay?" she asks, scrunching her nose. "We don't have to."

"No, I'm sorry. It's been a messed-up couple of days."

"You sure that's it?"

"Yeah, I'm fine."

She kisses him again, then leads him by the hand upstairs.

13

____

Hattie and Davis lie in bed catching their breath.

Slight glean of sweat. Heads fuzzy. Post-sex hazy smiles on their faces, the midday sun peeking through the blinds. Davis holds her hand, then looks to her. She winks and laughs like a teenager.

"See," she says, "everything's better."

Davis can't help but smile. He stops just short of cracking a make-up sex joke.

Looking to his wife, the memories of all they've done together rush into his head like a welcomed stampede. As he touches her face, he allows himself to appreciate where he is, what he has, and if only for a second, who he is.

He forces down the thoughts of Justin. Of Todd. Of LA.

"We should do this more," she says, turning on her side and facing him.

"Couldn't agree more."

"Should we put it on our calendars?"

"Jesus."

"I could." She giggles. "I'll send you an invite."

"Organizational Orgasms Review?"

"I'll bullet point positions and areas for improvement."

He shoves her. She laughs. It's a special laugh she gets when she really thinks something is funny. Davis gets lost in her eyes. Watching her laugh is one of his favorite things in life. He kisses her softly while lightly touching her back. Hattie releases a satisfied purr of a moan. With her mouth still close to his she says, "You trying to go again, sailor?"

"Please, this ain't college. There's no keg here."

Hattie breaks up. So does he.

"You know what would make this even better?" Hattie asks.

"What?" he asks, knowing damn well what's heading his way.

"Ice cream," she whispers sweetly. "Chocolate peanut butter."

Davis rolls his eyes then looks back at her. She giggles with a snort then covers her nose. He starts to laugh too, then stops.

Tilley's face flashes in his mind. He shakes his head.

"What?" Hattie asks, pulling back off his sudden break in expression. "You okay?"

Davis blinks. "Yeah, no I'm fine. Thought I was going to sneeze or something."

"Okay." She giggles again, pauses, then asks, "About that ice cream?"

———

"Yes, stolen," Davis says on the phone with the bank.

"Looks like there are several charges in Los Angeles."

"Yes, that's where I lost the card."

"We might not be able to reverse them all, but we will research the issue."

"Please do. I'd really appreciate it."

Davis drives with a small pile of credit cards stacked in the passenger seat. He's working his way through them while making his way to the store for ice cream. He has no idea how many Justin has infected with charges, so he's decided to call them all.

"Thank you." He hangs up as he parks his car. Davis feels a slight swell of pride over his small victory. Maybe he can get out of a few of the charges Justin rolled up on him. That's something at least. At this point Davis will take all the wins he can get, no matter the size.

Inside the store the dull murmur of nineties pop hits provides a soundtrack.

Davis slow-rolls his cart past the tall glass cases while he considers his ice cream options. The cold from the refrigerated section feels nice after the stress of the credit card conversation, and his perfect afternoon delight with Hattie. She said she wanted peanut butter and chocolate, not a shock, but he knows damn well it's not just a carton of peanut butter and chocolate. She's a big fan of the pro move of buying one pint of chocolate and one of peanut butter and then mixing them together at home. It's her thing, therefore it's his thing as well. He hates to admit, but it is better. He grabs a pint of each.

As he does, he feels the hairs on the back of his neck stand up on end.

He feels eyes watching him.

Studying him.

Spinning around, he finds nothing. No one is there.

Only an empty aisle and bad music. It's early afternoon on a weekday and the store as a whole is fairly empty. Davis looks down each side of the aisle, but doesn't see anyone. He knows he felt something, though. He also knows it's been a long couple of days. He's been through the ringer and he's drained and stressed beyond reason. Maybe he can let himself off the hook a little bit.

Shaking it off, he tells himself that he's only being paranoid. The vision of Tilley, the feeling like people are spying on him, they're all symptoms of what's happened to him. It's not real. Things are getting better. The noose, the one he's felt getting tighter and tighter ever since LA, is loosening.

If he can get a few of the charges reversed and work with Todd to get the business back on track, then maybe this will all be an unfortunate memory. He still feels guilty for the things he's told Hattie, but he did what he had to do. Would telling her about Justin, about Tilley, about any of it, would that make her feel any better? Would any of that make her feel any more secure about their financial situation?

No.

He never wants to put her through a money rollercoaster like that ever again.

I did what I had to do by not telling her.

Not proud of it, but it's been a necessary evil.

Davis knows he's a good guy. Far from perfect, but he's been a good husband and a good father. He's never lied to her before, not really. Never about anything serious. Never had a reason to, and this is a one-time thing, he tells himself. A bandage placed on what could have opened up into a very large and unmanageable wound. One that might not ever heal.

Davis's arm locks up straight as his cart stops as if it had brakes.

He looks up.

An attractive woman has both hands planted on the front of his cart, holding it tight, blocking him from moving forward. She's young, early twenties maybe, with fire-red hair, green eyes and a diamond-pierced nose. She cocks her head like a cocker spaniel then clucks her tongue, giving a dead stare into Davis's eyes.

He doesn't recognize her, but it seems she knows him.

"Hi," she says.

Davis swallows big. "Hello? Can I help you?"

The green-eyed beauty lets her eyes slip down to the contents of the cart. "You went with the mixing thing." She rubs her fingertips over the frosty ice cream pints, then licks her finger. "Smart boy."

Fear spikes deep inside of Davis. "Do I know you?"

"I'd say."

"I'm sorry." He stops, then starts again, pointing to the ice cream. "How do you know about—"

"Tilley told me." She gives him an eyebrow raise. "Told me all about you, lover boy." Then she turns, disappearing down another aisle as quickly as she appeared.

Once he's sure she's gone, Davis leans forward on the cart, letting his head rest on his arm as if he were just released from a crippling chokehold. His head starts spinning. He has no memory of ever meeting that woman, not even the vaguest memory of the green-eyed beauty. And he certainly doesn't remember telling Tilley anything about anything. His heart thumps like a jackhammer. He can feel sweat beading on his forehead as he runs through a new set of terrifying questions.

Was she in LA too?

She part of Justin's business?

Did he really tell Tilley about Hattie's after-sex ice cream? He's not sure he's told anybody about that. Ever. Why would he?

Why the hell would I tell Tilley?

He must have, though. How else would the green-eyed beauty know?

What else did I tell them?

He wants to throw up, but fights to hold it back best he can. All he wants to do is get the hell out of this store and get home. To crawl back in bed with his wife. He wants to hit reset and make this all go away. Start over. Somehow land in a place in time before LA.

Davis fumbles through his remaining cash at the register, his hands vibrating as he gives the cash over in a wad of bills. He doesn't even bother counting them out. The checkout guy looks at him sideways, not sure what his problem is, but also not caring enough to get involved.

Davis breathes in and out, gripping the two ice cream pints in his hands as he cuts through the parking lot, moving toward his car. The checkout guy offered a bag, but Davis ignored him, grabbing the ice-cold containers with his bare hands without a consideration.

The pints are beginning to drip, melting ice down his fingers. He sets the chocolate pint down on the roof of his car. He places his hand on the door handle, about to pull it open.

"Hey, Big Fun."

PART III

14

Davis spins around hard, almost tripping over his own feet.

That voice.

There's no mistaking that voice.

It's calm, cool and drenched in thick, syrupy confidence. Justin stands in front of him dressed in a sharp suit and tie. Everything about him sculpted. Perfect. Looks just as slick and cool as he did in LA when they first met.

Justin holds his hands out as if looking for a hug.

The green-eyed beauty waves at Davis as she walks up behind Justin and gives him a spank.

"Ooooh," Justin purrs. "Thank you, darling."

The green-eyed beauty blows him a kiss, then cracks open a forty-ounce malt liquor bottle as she keeps slinking down the parking lot toward the street. She tilts the beer back while walking away, never looking back.

Justin snickers, watching her leave, then leans against Davis's car.

Davis's eyes bounce. His heart skips a row of beats. He's frozen. Waiting for Justin's move.

"Hey, man, good to see you." He snaps his fingers, flashes a smile. "You've been ducking my calls."

Davis doesn't know what to say. His tongue is glued to the bottom of his mouth. His breathing has become hard to manage.

"Good job." Justin points to the ice cream. "The mixing thing. Smart move."

Davis's mind is mush, not able to process what's happened in the last few minutes.

How did they know I was here? Are they watching me?

The awkward silence between them mounts, but Justin never breaks eye contact. Cars come and go behind him, pulling in and out of parking places. Justin simply leans against the car, acting as if he's in the company of an old college buddy. People shuffle to and from the store. Justin pushes himself off the car, standing straight up with a bounce.

"Nothing?" Justin asks with a flicker of crazy dancing behind his eyes. "You got nothing for me?"

"What the hell are you doing here?"

"Shopping. Saying hello. So… hello."

"Are you following me?"

"I come here all the time. Not really, that's a lie."

"You charged a lot of money on my cards. What the hell is that all about?"

"Yeah, didn't want to go that way, but you really didn't leave me with many great options there, did ya?" Justin slips on his sunglasses. "Like I said, you keep ducking my communications."

"I don't remember anything—"

"It happens. I, however, remember quite a bit."

"What did you do to me?"

"I didn't come here to make a scene, Big Fun. Facts are facts, and the fact is you ran up a bit of tab. Big tab. Those charges? Those don't cover it all, not even close."

Davis's stomach balls up tight.

"See, that five thousand—just to pick one—that was, oh, let's call it a first installment."

"Installment?"

"Yes, yes, sir."

"How much?"

"Pardon?"

"How much to end this?"

"Did you not have a good time?"

"Jesus."

"Did you?"

"Come on, Justin."

"Did you have the time of your life?"

"How much?" Davis barks hard.

"Easy, Big Fun." Justin holds out his hand like a stop sign. He pauses, then puts up a finger acting like he's doing math on an imaginary chalkboard. "Looks like, maybe..." He carries the one. "Ten grand more."

Davis wants to break down in the middle of the parking lot.

He doesn't have it. Not sure where he could even pull that together. Still not sure he did anything wrong. The image of Tilley this morning doesn't help reassure him. His thoughts race. The debts he already owes. Todd. The business. Hattie. The money problems from the past. The girls. Air becomes hard to find as his chest tightens. His vision blurs.

"Big-time business man like you, solving the world's literary problems and such, ten grand should be in your damn couch cushions."

"Not that simple—"

"Could be. Could be simple, or get a little complicated."

"What's that mean?"

"Mean you could fucking pay me or things can get real weird real damn fast."

Justin's words are never spoken in more than a

conversational tone. His inflections aren't threatening. He never raises his voice. He simply opens his coat, revealing a brown leather shoulder holster.

Only there's no gun inside the holster.

Justin pulls out a phone instead.

Justin didn't make a show of it but it there's no doubt that he wanted Davis to see.

Does he want me to know there's gun that he usually carries?

Does he want me to know that's what's next?

"Or..." Justin taps his phone, "We can keep kicking each other in the balls via texts." He turns his phone over and over in his hands, letting his fingers glide over the glass. "These things are amazing, right? Phones today. The things they can pick up. The moments they can record." He lets his eyes meet Davis's. "Moments that can be shared."

His breathing all but stops.

Davis can only look at the phone, wondering what's on there.

Is the phone the real weapon he wants me to see?

"You really don't remember anything, do you?" Justin asks.

Davis shakes his head, voicing a "No" barely above a whisper.

"Wow. That must be frustrating." Justin slips the phone back into his shoulder holster. "Guess it'll be fun for you to see what happened that night. For everybody, I guess."

Davis has no intention of playing this game anymore. He has no idea what Justin has. He could be bluffing or maybe he's not. If all he wants is money, then Davis wants to end this, even if he knows money is the one thing he doesn't have.

"I can get you some of it," Davis spits out, trying to convince himself, hating himself for caving in like this, like he always does. "Half. I'll get you half."

"Half?"

Davis nods. The sweat is starting up again.

"As in, not all of it?"

"I'll get you five thousand—"

"Tomorrow."

"What?"

"You'll get me five thousand by tomorrow." Justin holds his eyes.

"I'll try, but you have to stop texting me."

Justin taps his chin, considers Davis's words. Then he turns, possibly thinking about his own before saying them. He lets his silence linger, creating a void in their conversation. Justin's way of letting Davis's imagination run wild with the possibilities of how Justin will respond, wanting Davis to start thinking about everything. Everything that could go wrong.

"Five grand tomorrow then," Justin finally says,

then turns, about to leave. He stops, turns back to Davis as if he forgot something. "You, man, you were a crazy one."

"What?"

"That night. You know, in LA?"

"Please." Davis now brought to begging. "Tell me what happened."

"The shit you did. Good God, man." Justin starts to laugh. "I've seen some wild stuff in this business of mine, but you? You surprised even me."

Davis feels his chest tighten even more. His throat closing.

Justin slows his laughing, studies Davis's expression with a squint. "Amazing. You truly don't remember a damn thing, do you?"

"No," Davis says harder, much more than a whisper this time.

Justin's face goes to stone in the blink of an eye. "Tilley? She's a good one. She knew the risks, but damn, bro."

"What?" Davis fumbles over his tongue. "What are you talking about?" His mind bends, trying to remember. He works to force-feed information back into his brain, desperate to recall the recent image of Tilley. Tries hard to make sense of what Justin just said to him.

"Is she okay?" he asks, struggling to control the shaking in his voice.

Justin places his finger to Davis's lips, shushing

him like a child. "Fire the wire to these instructions." Justin hands him a slip of paper with
banking instructions listed. "Do it fast, now."

Justin walks away.

"Your ice cream is melting, Big Fun."

15

Davis stumbles into his home.

"Hello," he calls out for Hattie.

Nothing.

He rushes upstairs, checking each room. His face and back are still slick with sweat from his encounter with Justin in the parking lot.

"Hello?"

The house is empty.

He looks to his phone; he has a recent missed call and a text from Hattie. He holds his breath, worried that Justin did something. Anything is possible now. Checking Hattie's text, he exhales, letting the weight of the universes leave him. For the moment at least.

sorry. had to run to the office. ice cream later?

Davis holds onto the railing of the stairs for balance as he makes his way downstairs. He puts the nearly-melted ice cream into the freezer and leans on the counter, letting his palms support him. His sight slides out of focus as he stares into the granite pattern of countertop. He breathes in slow and deep. In through his mouth and out through his nose. A technique he learned from a baseball coach years ago. Davis used to get so damned nervous before heading up to the plate. He always saw himself striking out before he even got there. As he works his breathing his brain begins to unspool, letting everything Justin told him data dump into his head at the speed of light.

Tilley.

What was Justin talking about?

What happened? Is he just screwing with my head?

Trying to get the money out of me?

More money.

He can't believe he gave in to Justin like that. Todd would have told him to go fuck himself or fought him right there in the parking lot. But what was Davis supposed to do? They could have slugged it out in front of the minivans, but what would that do? Real good chance Justin might have a gun. He doesn't seem the type, probably keeps a gun as a scare tactic, but Davis would rather not test it. There's no upside in any of that. Davis knows he had no play to make, but still hates what happened.

He knows this is all his fault anyway.

Davis tells himself he made a mistake. Convinces himself that he'll have to pay for it. That's how this all works. It's what he was always taught as a child: you screw up, you pay the price. *Own your shit*, his old man always told him. His old man also drank himself to death and had no less than three marriages.

He owned it all right. Right into the ground.

Davis reviews his finances in his head. It's creative financing, to be sure, but it can be done. Hattie will see it eventually, but right now he needs to manufacture time. He grabs his phone, swipes and taps, pulling up his bank account app. His eyes scan down the page, his lips moving as he works through the numbers.

It's not good. He's dry.

Davis has poured everything he has into the company. He financed part of the company by drawing cash from his personal credit cards, maxing out two of the three, then opening a couple more. He can still maybe scrape together around three thousand after the month's upcoming expenses, maybe, so he'll have to borrow the remaining two thousand from another card that Davis keeps hidden away from emergencies to cover Justin's money by tomorrow. He knows it's only a matter of time before the emails and calls about charging over his limit start rolling in. It's a damn miracle Justin was able to get the charges through in the first place.

He remembers his daughters' dance lessons are due in a week.

Hattie's car needs work.

The fence needs work. The numbers begin to spin again.

"Shit," he mutters to himself.

He doesn't know what to do. He can barely come up with the payment for tomorrow, if at all. How the hell is he going to pay the rest of it? A fear-tremor rattles him to the core.

Not long ago he poured everything into a company he cares for and deeply believes in. He didn't have any savings, but he didn't have any debt, and he had a lot of prospects in LA lined up. Things piled up. Unexpected startup costs popped up, as they always do, and Davis took some of it on with cards. Todd took on the rest, using his family nest egg. Now, it looks like Davis is going to owe a mountain of debt so he can pay a crazy person, and the business prospects are drying up left and right.

Hattie is going to kill him. This will be crushing to her. He's doing it again, something he promised he'd never do. The money spiral is gaining speed and he's dragging her deeper and deeper into it. Again.

How can he possibly hide all of this?

He taps and moves some money around, then

sends a money wire out to the instructions Justin gave him. Davis's stomach drops to the floor as the confirmation comes up. He can almost actually see the money fly away. He can see Hattie leaving with the girls.

He knows what he has to do. He hates it, but he has no other real options. Picking up his phone, he makes the call. One he should have made in the beginning.

"Todd?"

16

———

Davis stares into his swirling caramel-colored coffee as he speaks.

He avoids all eye contact as he tells Todd about LA. About what happened. About Justin. All of it, at least what he can remember.

Todd is pissed, oddly quiet at times, but he manages to be surprisingly compassionate. He doesn't yell or slam the table or litter the air with profanity or name-calling. He listens, face red as hell, but he listens to what Davis has to say and doesn't interrupt. Lets his friend and business partner unload his burden.

Davis finishes, ending the story with how Justin and the green-eyed beauty blindsided him at the grocery store.

Todd takes a sip of his coffee. Thinks. Considers. Picks through everything his friend has told him.

"Thoughts?" Davis asks with a crack in his voice. "Never seen you so damn quiet."

"Look, you fucked up. Not gonna lie to you. That much is certain," Todd says. "It happens. We can't undo any of that, so we need to focus on what we can control." He pauses, letting his ideas swirl. "So, the question really is what the hell do we do going forward?"

"I don't know. Just the money part of it has me scrambling. I'm tapped out. You know that. I put it all into the business."

Todd nods.

"I don't have a safety net like you. No family money. It's just me and Hattie, that's it."

Todd takes another sip of his coffee, listening, letting Davis unload.

"I don't know," Davis says, talking more to himself than Todd. "When we started this business all I wanted to do was build something, ya know? You and I were working at that shitty corporate hell, sitting in cubes, running spreadsheets and creating reports that nobody looked at. It was us making shit we didn't care about for people who didn't give a shit about seeing it." Todd snickers. "Remember training class?"

"Damn." Davis allows a smile to crack, remembering that's how they met in the first place. He hadn't thought about that in some time. "We came up with a product—"

"You. You came up with a product." Todd waves his hand. "I'm not smart enough for any of that genius crap."

"Whatever. We did it. We put together a product that could solve a problem and, yeah, make some money. Left that dump and started out on our own to do something, something new. Something we could be proud of, and in the process give corporate America the finger."

"Damn right."

"Now?" Davis leans back, looking out the window. "Now it's all going to hell, isn't it? Poof."

"No, the hell with that nonsense," Todd says. "We ain't done. Not by a long shot."

Todd leans in. Davis does too. This is the Todd he knows. The Todd he called. This is the Todd who solves problems. The Todd he needs.

"What this clown did is illegal, right?" Todd asks.

"Maybe."

"No maybe to it. I'll call the lawyer and figure this out."

"I can't pay for lawyers, man."

"I got this. There's a friend who owes me a favor. A kid I grew up with who would love to sink his teeth into this thing here. He'll consider it fun."

Davis feels some of the weight lift from his chest.

"I'm sorry, man," Davis says as the shame and guilt eases back to him. "I should have never let it get this far. Shouldn't have gotten the company involved."

"Davis—"

"I was just trying to do the right thing and take care of it all on my own."

"Of course. That's what you do. You always try to do the right thing. You try to carry the weight alone, even when you don't have to. That's what makes you Davis the Great."

Davis smiles big, remembering the first time Todd called him that.

Davis the Great.

It was when Davis showed him the first version of the software, the original, with bugs and all. Davis ran through his mini-pitch to Todd in such a blur he could barely get the words out fast enough. He was so excited, so filled with passion back then. Todd got wrapped up in his friend's enthusiasm immediately. They stayed up all night working through the business possibilities—a half-assed plan at best—talking through it all without taking a break, eating, or sleeping for that matter. They both walked into work the next day bleary-eyed from lack of sleep, but happy as hell. They quit that day.

Quit that corporate hell with punch-drunk smiles on their faces.

It was a great day.

Today, however, Davis is feeling far less great.

"It's going to be okay," Todd says, seeing it on Davis's face. "We'll get this right."

Davis nods, letting the warm coffee provide him some comfort.

"Just don't pay that asshole anything else. Let me see what I can do."

17

———

ON THE WAY HOME, Davis replays his conversation with Todd over again in his head.

We'll get this right.

It's going to be okay.

Davis the Great.

He does feel better, but he's not sure why. Nothing's really changed. Maybe simply talking it through with someone helps. Maybe bringing Todd into the picture helps ease some of the isolation he was feeling. Bringing a friend on board has its own comfort. The simple fact there's some kind of plan in place doesn't hurt either. Davis knows the lawyer buddy Todd is talking about, knows the kind of attack dog he is and what he's capable of doing. There's a level of comfort that comes from knowing that guy is on the case.

Maybe this *can* work out. Perhaps this can still be okay.

Maybe.

Perhaps.

Davis turns up the radio, letting an old Pixies tune take him back to a less complicated time. The music helps him take a mental break from the here and now. Takes him by the hand to a place that always brings a smile to his face. This song, it reminds him of Hattie, of when they were young. Before stress. Before all the pressures that come with adult life. The tugging and pulling of money problems, the house, and the scheduling constraints that come with having children in your life. They love the kids more than anything, and wouldn't change it for anything, but man, they do cut into your life as a couple.

No doubt.

He remembers them being born. Separate, tiny little people coming into the world without a care. The days of the four of them living in that tiny apartment. Scraping money together, saving a penny here and there. Coupons. Working over-time. Hattie going back to work. Davis's first busi-ness failing. The debt. The crushing stress and strain of debt.

They pulled themselves out of it, but it left a mark. A scar that will never fade.

It hit Hattie the hardest. Her feeling of safety

was rattled hard during that time, but to her credit, when Davis told her he wanted to leave his cushy corporate gig to start this new thing with Todd, she didn't flinch. She did not hesitate. Her support was immediate and unwavering.

"Do it," was all she said.

He'll never forget that.

Davis remembers again how he told her it would be different this time. How he promised he had learned some hard lessons from the first business, and things would be so much different this time. The experience forged a new mindset: he would never put them in that position again, would not let them fall deep in the hole like last time.

She'd smiled, held his face and kissed him, but Davis felt her concern. Maybe he imagined it, or perhaps he projected it onto her, but he could tell she was scared.

She was right.

She usually is.

Davis lets the music of the Pixies wash over him. He bobs his head slightly to the beat, hoping this all works out. Hoping Todd and his attack dog can shake Justin's jaws loose from his throat, that this will all fade into the background. Hoping this will all go the hell away.

He doesn't know if his family can take it this time. Not sure if Hattie would be willing to live through that again. He can't blame her. She works hard and makes it all look easy. Davis knows it's not.

Hattie the Great, he thinks.

He stops at a red light. He turns the Pixies up even louder as he leans back into the headrest of his Accord, letting the beats and words fill in the empty spaces of his broken thinking.

A BMW pulls up next to him. A window rolls down. The green-eyed beauty starts singing the same Pixies song at the top of her lungs from the passenger seat. Justin is behind the wheel, bobbing his head ever so slightly with the music.

Davis's knuckles pop as he grips the steering wheel tight.

Justin fakes shock to see Davis, then waves. The green-eyed beauty sings louder. Justin holds up a brown shopping bag. It has a colorful store logo and name printed big across it.

Davis's eyes go wide.

Justin is holding a bag from the clothing company Hattie works for.

"Did you—" Davis calls out.

The light turns green and the BMW takes off with the sound of the green-eyed beauty's singing trailing off into the distance.

18

DAVIS STEPS INTO THE HOUSE.

He's met immediately by Hattie. She's holding her phone. He can see she's rattled. Her eyes are red, with the hint of tears in the corners. Tears not caused by sadness. She's frustrated, angry. Forget that, she's mad as hell. Davis's mind races through the possibilities of what conversation she had on that phone. Considering he saw Justin with a bag from her employer, she could be angry about a lot of things.

None of them registering as good.

He fumbles through that list, ripping through the possibilities in his strained mind. He tries best he can to pick them off one by one while forming some form of explanation, but it's a lost cause. The list is long, the mountain high and steep. He's losing the will to fight the fight.

He opens his mouth, seconds from unloading everything he's got crammed and jammed into his mind. Wanting to let it flow freeform out into the space between them. Let his words somehow bridge the gap that's begun between them. Something in him stops.

He knows the truth is poison now. He's gone too far.

He closes his mouth, deciding not to try and solve this at all. He knows her better than that. He fights every instinct he has to try and make this better before listening. That's always his initial reaction to her being upset—fix it. He knows he needs to hear her out before talking. Waiting for what seems forever, he waits for her to talk first.

"My card got declined," she says, waving her phone at him. "What the hell?"

"I canceled the cards," Davis says, scrambling to find a logical response. "I told you I was going to—"

"Okay, but—."

"It's being taking care of."

"I called the card company, Davis. The card we keep in case of emergency? We're late on the girl's dance lessons so I tried to use it." Hattie sighs, shaking her head. "They told me about the cash advance you made. That pushed us over the limit. What's going on?"

He knows he had to do it. No choice.

No play. Justin had to be fed something to hold him off.

Things can get real weird real damn fast.

Justin's words dig in. The way he said it.

The ever-so-casual flash of the gun holster.

The less-casual threat of the information contained on his phone.

Davis felt like he needed to buy some time, and he was out of options. Davis can see the questions forming in Hattie's mind. The doubt building is now showing in her eyes. He knows she loves and trusts him, but she has limits, and those limits have taken a massive beating lately.

"I had to it. The business needed quick cash—"

"Dammit, Davis."

"I know. I know. But it's for that potential account in LA. We'll get a quick turnaround on the money."

Hattie rocks on her heels, processing, but not giving in either.

Davis feels the nagging guilt of his words tugging at his insides, but stuffs it down. He's committed now, no turning back now, he has to work the narrative he's constructed.

"I'll pay it off immediately. I just needed the float until the client money comes in. It should be really soon."

"And Todd couldn't float it?"

"Todd?" Davis searches for an excuse. "He's tied up in some house flipping thing or whatever."

Hattie and Davis both know Todd has deep family money.

"I'll take care of it. Won't take long. Couple of days," Davis says.

"That's all?"

"That's all. Soon as their first payment comes in it'll more than cover it."

Hattie nods. She believes him. Davis can see it in her eyes, and it kills him.

The gap grows wider.

"Okay," she says. "I'm going to pick up the girls. I'll figure out something with the dance lessons."

Davis exhales, knows he dodged a big bullet. He can't keep this up. It's going to rip apart his life and destroy his relationship with Hattie, if it hasn't already. But he has no idea what to do now. It's all spinning out of control. He's spiraling down, the lies stacking up high one on top of another, and he doesn't know if he can stop. Like cards shuffling together, the things he's told her are mixing. Hard to tell where the truth ends and the lies start. All he knows for sure is that telling Hattie everything now will only make things far worse. She will never trust him again. How could she? Why should she?

Todd needs to come through and help him fix this. He has to.

Davis's phone buzzes.

The text from Justin reads:

thx for the $... excellent start

19

———

New day.

Feels like the same day all over again.

The texts from Justin fire off at a relentless clip as Davis helps Hattie get the girls off to school and get her off to work. Every buzz of the phone feels like an earthquake.

Davis counts five in the last thirty minutes. He's stopped reading them. They read friendly, for the most part, but Davis feels a bite behind every character sent. He knows Justin chooses each word carefully. There is only one central theme, one message really. They are all about money. The money Davis owes. Hammering him over and over again with dollar amounts owed.

The phone buzzes again. Davis ignores it again. He's moved on to his coffee shop slash office. He sits, unpacking his tools: his laptop, along with a yellow legal pad and a pen. He selects the same table every time, one at the back that gives him a view of the place. It's near the bathroom and he still gets a nice view out the window. When he meets Todd here he chooses a different table. He likes to separate the two.

He sits alone with his headphones planted in his ears checking emails, pouring over numbers, stuffing work into his brain while trying to stop thinking about Justin and the LA problem. He reviews the pitch deck he and Todd put together. It's a good one.

Still, it's the one Davis completely screwed the pooch on the other day. Somehow, going over the product details soothes him, makes him feel happy. Proud. In all this, he had forgotten that they have done something kind of great. It's a good product that can help people. The idea came to Davis while they were working at that corporate hell where he became friends with Todd. They were both buried deep in an email chain between them and some other colleges about a bitch of a project that was coming up.

Davis can't even remember what it was about now. Didn't care then, cares even less now. The emails went on for days and days and days. The back and forth soaked up hours and hours of productivity. It was sad. Pathetic. Mainly because it didn't have to. No reason for it all to drag on that long. It was beyond dumb. The bottleneck that brought everything to a crawl was so minor it could've been solved in a snap. There was a simple misunderstanding that all stemmed from the original email sent by the team lead.

This idiot.

This *leader*.

His words weren't clear. That's all. He simply could not communicate his thoughts to his people. The words he used were too passive. His email was thick, dense with walls of words that didn't mean anything. They all circled around the issue, poked at the intent, but inside that hurricane of words there was no point or any sort of actionable item. Like a thousand toothless sharks swimming in circles around people holding buckets of fish. No bite. No way of doing anything.

Davis combed over the emails and discovered a pattern. A pattern of bullshit, Todd called it. This bullshit pattern could have been solved with a simple algorithm. A bullshit detector, Todd called it.

Davis spent nights, weekends, early mornings, and burned sick days and holidays perfecting his algorithmic solution. He went through countless versions. Started, scrapped one completely, started over and then trashed that one too. Each time he learned something though, and he kept building on the backs of those mistakes until he had something. Something great.

His brainy bullshit detector.

Davis and Todd tested it on company emails on his laptop at night when he got home, even the ones from that same idiot team lead that started it all, and Davis's software worked time and time again. Davis's little invention was able to distill, digest, edit and suggest ways to make written communication more effective. He and Todd did some research about the skill of writing and how it has diminished greatly over the years. Social media, emails, and texts have broken what used to be a fundamental skill for the workforce. For people in general.

The art of written communication is falling apart.

One point of research suggested that what we are taught in school about how to write papers, for example, was broken to begin with and probably should've never been taught in the first place. The structure of a school essay was designed so teachers can grade a large number of them easily, so they follow a certain A, B, C pattern, usually with a mandatory word count. This leads to, in the researcher's opinion, students who believe they can get a better grade by filling sections with, well, bullshit. It encourages students to dump endless streams of words onto a page in order to hit a mark.

These students are rewarded with good grades. These students then become adults in the workforce. Those adults then become idiot members of management, and in turn, send out emails that suck and lack any kind of clarity. This causes an entire organization to come to a grinding halt as others try to figure out what the hell is going on. Add to all this the technology aspect of face-to-face business interaction deteriorating, and you've got a problem with a fundamental human need.

Communication.

This is what Davis created, what Davis and Todd set out to start a business around. It requires some salesmanship—not as simple as pitching a new flavor of chips—but when clients understand it they buy it and love it. They love it because it works. The first day they started, Davis said he was scared as hell to start the business. Todd was too, but he said something Davis will never forget.

"The hell with it. When you're all out of good ideas you've got to go with the bad ones."

Davis's phone buzzes. At first glance Davis shrugs it off as another Justin text, but it's a call this time. Flipping his phone over, he sees it's coming from the company he met with in town. The one where his presentation was such a disaster.

Davis's heart jumps. His hands shake.

Did they change their mind?

He did leave hard copies of the presentation

behind. Maybe they looked it over and wanted to talk some more. He clears his throat, then answers the call.

"This is Davis."

"Well hello, Davis. This is Justin."

Davis feels his emotions slip away from him, peel off from his body like meat from the bone in a boiling pot. As if hope was on the tips of his fingers, then he had to watch that hope slip and fumble, falling away from him.

"Hello?" Justin says. "This is how I have to get ahold of you now? You know how much shit I had to feed the gay admin to get to use this phone?" Justin pauses for effect. "A lot, Davis. It was a lot of shit."

"What do you want?"

"What the hell do you think? Come on, you're better than that, man."

"I paid you what we agreed on." Davis sees the people around him are giving him looks. His voice must have shot up. He didn't even notice. Getting ahold of himself he lowers his voice. "I need a couple of days for the next installment, that's all."

"Any idea how long it's going to take for you to pay me back at this sad-ass rate?"

"Justin. You need to understand—"

"No, pretty sure I don't *need* to do a damn thing."

"I'm doing my best. My wife doesn't trust me.

My accounts are dry. My business is five seconds away from not being a business anymore. This is all I can do. Period."

Davis thinks of Todd and the lawyer he's talking to. Todd said not to pay Justin any more money. Davis is struggling hard to buy himself time here.

"That's it, Big Fun?" Justin says. "You done with the talky talk?"

"I don't know what else to tell you."

There's a pause. A wall of silence from Justin's side of the conversation.

Davis grips the phone, squeezing trying to give himself some form of comfort.

Justin begins clucking his tongue, a now familiar sound Davis is learning to hate. Seconds crawl. Time seemingly stops. Justin whispers some things Davis can't quite make out. Maybe he's counting. Maybe he's reciting something. Lyrics to a song. Davis can't even tell if Justin is using words or just gibberish.

"You're right," Justin finally says. "We should really figure this the hell out. It's silly really. Hate to make your life any worse than you already have."

The coldness in his voice shakes Davis to the bone.

"Justin?"

He's hung up.

Davis looks around the coffee shop. Everybody

going about their day, moving through their lives. Some are laughing and enjoying conversations with friends. Others have their noses buried in books, phones or laptops. Davis's envy for them burns. He possibly hates them. Wishes he were one of them. He wishes he could go back to being a guy at a coffee shop, back to being the Davis before all of this.

Before LA.

Before Justin.

Davis drives home, trying to let his conversation with Justin fade into the background. He listens to a podcast about fantasy football. Tries silence. Tries some music. None of it is working. The conversation sticks. Echoing like a hammer driving nails in a vacant house.

It was the tone Justin used more than the words. It was how he talked to Davis that has him worried. Justin wasn't mad or nervous or anything vaguely like it. He had complete control at all times. Never once did he raise his voice or fumble over his words. It was like everything he said was carefully scripted ahead of time. Like it was curated by an expert of calm and cool, then the lines were fed to Justin so he could repeat them to Davis.

Davis walks into the house. The kids and Hattie won't be home for a while, so Davis kicks off his shoes and flops onto the couch, still trying to get his head around the call with Justin. Normally he'd appreciate the time to himself, but not today. He'd love to have the distraction of his family right now. Justin's words still echo in his ears.

We should really figure this the hell out.

Hate to make life any worse than you already have.

The phone buzzes. This time it is a text from Justin.

Davis lets his finger hover over his phone, not wanting to see what is waiting for him. Not after that last conversation. Not wanting to see the message that's hanging in digital purgatory, begging to be seen. It's going to be about money that he doesn't have. Like the worst bill collector in history. Davis pulls his hand back, but he knows he has no choice.

He taps the screen. No words in the text.

None needed.

There's only a single image. A picture of Davis smiling wide, holding a bottle of Knob Creek, surrounded by women. Gorgeous women. Some topless. Some in lacey bras and panties. Davis doesn't recognize any of them. Tilley's not there, and neither is the green-eyed beauty. He stands up, pacing the room now.

Phone buzzes. His shaking finger taps the screen faster this time.

Another pic comes through. He almost drops his phone.

It's an image of Davis kissing Tilley. Neither is wearing clothes. Naked bodies wrapped around each other, his hand squeezing her breast.

Another text. This one does contain words.

did u have the time of your life?

20

———

THE PHONE SLIPS from his fingers, falling to the floor.

The dog sniffs at it.

Davis leans back against the wall, his face void of expression, as if it melted away. He can't focus on a single thought as they pop like popcorn bouncing off the walls of his skull.

How can I not remember?

Not any of that?

It was like looking at someone else in those pictures. Someone else who'd stolen his face, taken over his body. That can't be him. How could it be?

His life is ruined. He's completely undone his place in this world in a single night. Shattered it all into a million pieces, with no hope of putting it back together. Not if those pictures get out.

Davis slides down the wall, taking a seat on the

floor while staring out into the void, a place far away, deep out into the universe that only he can see. His eyes slip over to his phone on the floor where he dropped it. He feels something inside him unhinge, like the stitching that's holding him together is tearing.

Davis dives forward, grabbing the phone. He's now lying flat on his stomach as he frantically dials Justin. The dog licks his face. Davis pushes him aside.

The phone rings.

"Pick up," Davis says through grinding teeth.

The rings sound one after the other.

"Come on."

Davis stands up as the phone continues to ring and ring. He hangs up then calls Justin again. Another chorus of empty rings with no answer. Davis slams the phone down on the kitchen counter.

"I was just talking to you!" he screams.

He starts pacing like a madman, pausing only to wrap his face in his hands. Veins plump up on the sides of his neck. Another one rises up on his forehead. His skin feels hot, like he's burning from the inside out. He hates himself for what he's done.

The lying to Hattie.

All he's now laid on Todd.

Davis knows now that he did do something. Before he saw those pictures, he didn't know and he could live in the delusion that he was innocent in all this. He was safe in not knowing.

Now he does.

Hattie trusted him.

Todd is trying to help.

Davis is void of innocence. He's dragging them both down into the muck right along with him. The speed of his pacing escalates. Manic movement back and forth, turning here and there, zigzagging across the living room with no real pattern or reason for his motions.

The dog follows him, thinking it's a game.

Davis's mind races, running through the things he saw in those pictures. The things he's done that his broken mind doesn't recall. Things he should have done differently. He should have just gone up to his room and stayed there. Left Justin and Tilley at the bar. He's a good person. A good man. That much he knows. At least he thought he knew it. One simple misstep. Can one damn mistake undo an entire lifetime of good?

He stops cold in the middle of the living room off a sound from the kitchen. The dog stops too. The phone is buzzing. Davis races over to the kitchen, snatching it from the counter. It's Justin.

"Sorry I missed your call, Big Fun," Justin says to him. "I was taking a dump."

"Why the hell are you doing this? What's the

point?" Davis asks. "I've already agreed to pay you—"

"I've upgraded your entertainment package. Your bundle has been upsized."

Davis's face drops.

"See, if you'd paid me in the first place, meaning not ignoring me like you did, we could've stayed with Package B. But *because* you thought silence was golden, and it's not by the way, I've had to move you up to Package A."

"Justin—"

"Hey, hey." Justin snaps his fingers, shifting fast to a hard, cold tone. "You had a chance. My turn now, and you need to listen to the shit I have to say."

Davis takes in a deep breath.

"Listening ears on?"

"Yes," Davis says, barely above a whisper.

"Good. Where the hell was I? Oh yeah. Package A is actually a great value for you. It's only a grand a week for the rest of your life."

Davis's eyes glaze over. The words *for the rest of your life* hang in the air. He doesn't even try to do the math on that. Justin could have said a million a week, wouldn't matter. Davis can't pay either one. Davis's mouth goes dry. His head rattles as he feels words swell to the back of his tongue, unable to bring them all the way out.

Justin clucks his tongue, pauses, then starts up again.

"Now, a grand a week isn't nearly enough for me to live on." Justin sighs. "But I don't need to, because each new Package A that I sell only adds to my portfolio. I don't need to tell you about the need for multiple streams of income."

Davis holds on to the kitchen counter for support. He thinks of his first conversation with Justin, back in LA. He told Davis about how he wouldn't believe how many *packages* he sold to Hollywood, Fortune 500 companies, athletes and so on. And now he has Davis. Davis the customer. The client.

"You might want to do what past customers have done—use that financial weight to fuel you."

Davis tries again to get out some words, but all he can manage comes out as a frail whisper of noth-ingness.

"Turn that new thousand a week payment need into desire, a burning desire for you to come up with a new way to make an additional thousand a week over the top of your living expenses. I want you to live, of course. How else am I going to make my money?" Justin giggles. "It'll force you to be creative. In turn, you'll come up with something much bigger than a grand a week. Smart kid like you? You'll hatch a new million-dollar idea that changes everything."

"I –" Davis finally gets out.

"Wait, wait, wait. I got it. Damn, man, this is good," Justin says. "You're going to dig this one. New package, just for you. A package with a one-time exit plan. A balloon payment, if you will. You ready for this, Big Fun?"

Davis sits down, letting the deafening silence swell, not wanting to say a thing. He can't wait to hear what Justin has to say, but doesn't want to hear what's next.

"You kill someone of my choosing and I forget the whole goddamn enchilada."

Davis closes his eyes. Bad went to hopeless in no time flat.

"I'm kidding. Kinda. Maybe. Not really, but think about it anyway," Justin says, then hangs up.

21

———

Davis flies out the front door.

His eyelids stretch wide, tears forming in the corners. He walks slowly, clumsy and barefoot, down his neighborhood street, ignoring the heat of the concrete. The sun beats down on him. Sweat begins to bead on his forehead.

Dead man walking, he thinks.

His phone hangs from his lifeless arm. This phone, it holds all his pain and his salvation at the same time. Everything that is wrong is in this hunk of plastic. The texts. The emails. The pictures. It also contains the only hope for answers. For resolution. He lifts the phone and spins through his recent calls. Stabbing a finger, he selects a number.

"Hey—" Todd answers.

"Tell me you've got something."

"Nothing good."

"What?" Davis barks, spit flying from his lips.

"Davis, you've got to bring it down."

"Are you kidding me? Did you really just say that? This is getting out of control."

"What happened?"

Davis takes a deep breath. "He's got pictures. Pictures, Todd."

"Okay, that's not great but—"

Davis's phone buzzes.

It's another text from Justin. Another picture. This one is worse. Hands. Mouths. Tongues twisting with several women. Another one comes in. Then another and another. The pictures are escalating. Each is the same, and yet different at the same time. Each one is a graphic image of Davis getting a blowjob, only each picture shows him with a different woman. Women Davis doesn't recognize. One with pink hair. One blonde. One Hispanic and another Asian.

Each picture showing him a sexual past he does not recall.

A spectator to his own pornography.

"What is going on?" Davis hears Todd ask through the speaker as his eyes slip in and out of focus while staring down at the texts that keep rolling in.

"Are you still there?"

Davis thinks about throwing the phone in the gutter and just running away. Running hard and fast and continuing to run until his lungs collapse. Until his legs wilt, give out, fold underneath him. Running away until he's so far gone that none of this matters. Hattie and the girls would be better off. Better without a man like him in their lives.

"Davis!" Todd yells.

Another text buzzes. The sound stabs like a cold blade.

none of these look like Hattie

Davis wants to throw up. It's not only the words in Justin's text, it's what's lurking behind them. He's telling Davis things in the spaces between the words. Saying he'll be happy to show these to Hattie. That he knows what Hattie looks like. That he knows how to reach her.

Is he following her? Watching her? Watching the house? My family?

Davis's world stops spinning. Everything becomes very clear, very fast. He raises the phone. "This has to stop, now."

"Okay. Take a deep damn breath—"

"The hell with that shit." Davis stops, completely unaware there's a world around him. "He's going to come after my family. Hattie, the girls."

Todd pauses. Resets. "Okay, listen. I talked to the lawyer."

"And?"

"And it's not great. Extortion, and now black-mail, yes, that's all illegal, but that wouldn't stop Justin from releasing all that anyway. And, just thinking out loud here, now we don't know what else he has."

Davis looks to the sky, letting the sun beat down on his sweaty face and neck.

"Davis, we need to think about something else here."

"What?"

"We need to think about the company, too."

A shudder rattles through Davis.

"We don't know what that guy can do to the company. We have no idea what he has."

"He showed me—"

"Do you know he showed you everything?"

Davis doesn't answer.

"Do you know he doesn't have other stuff?"

Davis breathes in deep, closing his eyes. "No."

"If we don't know what else he's got, then how do we know what he can tie to the company. If he releases a bunch of sick shit and that all gets linked to our company—"

Honk!

A car is behind him.

Davis wandered into the middle of the street and is standing there like a crazy person. He waves the car around then walks over to the side of the street and takes a seat on the curb. In all of this happening to him, he didn't even think about the company. Didn't consider the potential damage it might cause. The possibility that he's put Todd and the company in jeopardy. The thought that he could bring the whole thing down with his one reckless night in LA is crushing.

Davis thought selling the company would be a sign of failure. He didn't want to do it. He let his ego cloud his judgment. If he had let Todd do that, hell, if he'd just heard the offer, maybe this would be different. If he had agreed to sell, none of this would have happened. They'd both be out, richer and not knee-deep in this disaster. It would have brought the security that Hattie has always wanted. The kind he could never give, always falling just short.

Davis feels a tremor rattle through his body as he understands what he's done. The realization he has destroyed everything is crushing. His actions, his mistakes, his pride, his stupidity have ruined everything for everybody. Even the idea is too much to bear. He'll never forgive himself.

"We've had that deal in our back pocket. I know you don't like it, but if that gets compromised by some freaky shit, then that deal is gone in the wind."

"I don't want to sell, Todd. I don't but—"

"I know you don't. I get it, but it's a nice parachute out if we decide we want to cash out. Right?"

"Yes." Davis barely gets the word out.

"Davis." Todd stops, then starts again. "The lawyer suggested something. It's a little out there."

"What?"

"A private investigator. He thinks we should bring in someone who'll dig into this Justin guy and tell us what's up with him. Maybe shake his tree a little bit."

"Okay," Davis says, willing do anything at this point. "Does he know somebody?"

"He does. I just need to give him the green light."

Davis rubs his face. "Do it."

"Good," Todd says. "Why don't you get out of town while this is going on?"

"Where?"

"I don't know. Go to that place of Hattie's, her uncle's place by the lake."

"Her parents'."

"Whatever. Take Hattie and girls out there for a while. That Justin guy won't be able to find you out there. Then we can get the lawyer and the detective to work this thing out."

Davis lets the idea roll around in his head.

"Tell Hattie you want to get some work done, need a change of scenery. It's not a lie; you need to rework the security patch for next month anyway. Two birds."

Davis knows Todd's right.

He doesn't know how he's going to sell it to Hattie.

22
____

"Can we go to the cabin?" the girls ask, bouncing in circles around Hattie's knees. "Please, please, please."

Hattie looks to Davis with a grin.

How the hell is she supposed to say 'no' to this?

"Really?" she says, still eyeing Davis.

"Come on, it'll be good for us. We can get out of town for a bit. I need to work on some things."

"You can't work here? What about my work?"

"You work from home all the time."

"It's not like that and you know it."

"Just for a few days."

"And them?" she asks, looking toward the girls.

"They're off on Monday and Tuesday for teachers' service days, so they'd only be really out for like a day or two."

"Yeeessss!" the girls squeal.

Davis has boxed her into a corner and she feels it.

"Why can't you work here, again?" she asks. "You do it all the time, too."

Davis resets, knowing he has to go deeper with this. He can see it in her eyes that she's not going to simply cave on this.

"This new client," he says.

"The potential LA one?"

"Yes," he says, feeling the twist in his gut. "They want all new slides. New reporting. They're going to be a high-maintenance pain in the—" He stops himself and plays the final word to the girls. "Butt."

They giggle off the pure joy that comes from the word *butt*. Nothing funnier than a good butt joke at their age.

Hattie smiles, shaking her head while watching her daughters enjoy the show. Davis takes a beat and looks over his family. He can't help but let the idea of losing this slip into his mind. The idea that Justin could infect their lives and turn this all to stone. All this could be over, taken away. Davis knows Todd is right. He has to do this, get out of town for few days. If he can get Hattie to go along with the cabin idea, then he can buy some time and this can still all work. It doesn't have to end in doomsday. They can still be rid of Justin, all of it.

He can put LA behind him forever. He can still hold on to what's good.

Moisture floods the corners of his eyes as he watches their faces.

Can one mistake undo a lifetime of good?

He turns to Hattie. Takes a deep breath.

"If I can get this right," Davis continues, "if I can turn this around, we can be good. Things can be okay."

Hattie sees the emotion all over her husband's face. This means something to him. Not sure why, but there's something going on inside her husband. This sudden trip to the lake, for whatever reason, means an awful lot to him.

Davis keeps his eyes on hers, hopes she'll write it off as his passion for the business.

"Okay," she says, holding his hand. "Let's go to the lake, I guess."

The girls almost explode from the floor, dancing like little crazy people.

Davis smiles, exhales, squeezes her hand.

The dog barks, dancing along with the girls.

"The dog comes too," Hattie says.

Davis tries to counter.

She puts up a hand. "Nonnegotiable."

23

———

THE SUN HAS JUST BEGUN the process of lighting up the day.

Davis drives the winding back roads, cutting through the countryside heading to Lake Oswego, leaving the Portland suburbs in the rearview mirror. The girls have calmed down since they left Beaverton. It took a while, but they've retreated deep into their tablets. Hattie and Davis both wish they didn't spend as much time with their faces buried in the abyss of *the screens*, but they don't know what to do about it. They monitor the time the best they can, try to teach good habits, but they know small screens aren't going away. Not anytime soon. Parenting in today's world is a constant evolution, not an exact science by any stretch.

The dog barks like a bastard.

Davis's teeth grind.

Hattie laughs. She loves it when the dog gets on his nerves. Davis secretly loves it too. He loves the game of acting like he hates the dog, but they both know he loves the damn, dumb fur bag. Once the dog lets it go, Hattie holds Davis's hand, letting her fingers loosely lock with his. He smiles, gives them a gentle squeeze.

The drive itself is oddly relaxing. Calming.

A chance to get out of his own head.

Davis and Hattie spend a nice moment with the radio off letting only the sound of the tires gripping the road fill the car. The kids have their headphones on so the two of them can simply sit, holding hands, watching the gorgeous trees and countryside fill their vision. A quiet moment of affection. Something that gets missed too easily during the chaos of life.

This is as relaxed as Davis has been in days. At least since before LA.

He hasn't thought about Justin, the pictures, what Todd is doing, or any of it for a solid hour and it feels pretty nice. He turns to Hattie, catching a quick glance without her noticing. She's holding his hand while resting her head on the coolness of the window, watching the world roll by with an ever-so-slight grin on her face. There's such a look of peacefulness on her pretty face. A face he's known since college. A woman he's spent most of his life loving.

"I'm glad we're doing this," she says, barely above a whisper.

"Me too."

Hattie leans back over toward his side of the car and rests her head on his shoulder as he drives. Davis feels a light flutter in his chest like he did back when they were younger. It surprises him a bit. After all these years, she can still do that to him.

Tilley's face streaks across his mind.

The pictures.

He imagines her scream ringing out.

Davis's shoulder tenses up. He shakes his head, trying to remove the unwanted thoughts and images from his head. Hattie jerks her head from his shoulder, giving him a confused look, then leans back toward the window. He wants to reach out and tell her that it's not her. She's done nothing wrong, nothing to earn any of this.

There's nothing for him to say.

The tires roll as silence fills the car again.

This time, only a little colder than before.

———

ONCE THEY REACH THE CABIN, Davis begins unpacking the car while Hattie and the girls run toward the lake house. It's an older place that's been kept up nice over the years by Hattie's family.

They've done well for themselves and share the house with Hattie and her sisters whenever they can. They've been generous toward Davis and Hattie in particular, with the lake house and other things, helping them out of some tight financial spots.

Davis often wonders if her family shakes their head at the decisions Hattie has made. Her decision to marry Davis. Their financial rollercoaster. How their little girl could have done better, and how their granddaughters are being raised. The risks he's taken. Do they think he's careless, foolish or brave?

Davis brought her parents up during one of their darker money times. He pushed the conversation to places he shouldn't have. The pressure had gotten to him and he'd had a couple of beers, said some things he wished he hadn't.

She cried, telling him that her family loved him and would never be that petty, but Davis knows different. He could see it on her father's face when they went to her parents' house that one Thanksgiving. It was only a flash, but Davis caught it in the look he gave him.

My little girl deserves more. More than you can give.

Davis grabs the last bag from the car, setting it on the ground. He does love this house. He just wishes he could provide one of his own for his family. Deep down inside he knows Hattie doesn't care, that she's okay with things, but it still bothers him. Hattie makes good money and Davis doesn't mind, as some men do, but he still has some of that male pride that eats at him from time to time. The ancient idea that he should be the breadwinner. He knows it's stupid, especially in this modern day, but it's still there. His mind slips back to the business. Money, always back to the money, then to Todd.

Then to Justin.

He's had his phone on Do Not Disturb the whole ride. He doesn't want to check it, but knows he has to.

The girls are already running and screaming like the little crazy people they are. Up and down they race on the long dock that stretches out into the lake like a runway.

Davis pulls out his phone. A chill rolls up his spine, tickling the hairs on the back of his neck. He knew damn well there would be texts, messages from Justin, but it's the number of them that's got him frozen. The volume and velocity is stunning.

He can hear the thump-thump, pat-pat of his daughters' feet on the dock. A joyous sound that's competing with the unwelcome, hard beating in his chest.

There are over forty texts, all from Justin. Davis scrolls through the messages, scanning the words as they blur past his straining eyes. Not all the words land. His mind steamrolls past the point of absorbing it all. It's too much to take in. The crushing, crashing characters jamming together to form words designed to intimidate him.

Constructed to weaken.

To generate fear.

Some of the texts are filled with profanity. Packed with hard words and harsh, blunt sentences. Some of them seem carefully crafted by Justin in order to sound friendly, even forgiving, but they're all variations of the first message. A single underlying theme.

r u avoiding me?

The first ten were actually that very same message over and over again.

r u avoiding me?

r u avoiding me?

r u avoiding me?

Streams and waves of characters saying the same thing, one after another.

Davis wants to call Todd. Right now. He wants to hear that everything is under control. That he has nothing to worry about, that people are on it, that this will go away soon. He wants a friendly voice to tell him that this is going to end. Davis is out of town, out of physical reach from Justin, but not from the psychological death grip that keeps getting tighter and tighter by the second.

The sound of the girls running back and forth along the dock snaps him out of it.

"I hope they wear themselves out," Hattie says, walking toward him.

Davis almost drops his phone but manages to pocket it. Quickly he covers his rocketing anxiety. He's not sure what she's said in the last few minutes. He hopes she hasn't noticed his mental distance.

"What?" he asks.

"Them. Our children. I hope they burn off some of that car ride energy and wear themselves out."

"Oh right, yeah," Davis says, his mind fumbling. "They don't wear out."

"True." She hugs her shoulders. "It's chilly out here. Coffee?"

"Sure, that sounds good."

Hattie nods, grabs a couple of bags, and kisses him on the cheek. Her soft lips feel like a bee sting. Maybe it's the nerves or perhaps the guilt, but he's never felt that way before. Never jolted by a kiss from Hattie. Davis tries not to jump back from her, instead finds a forced smile. Hattie walks away toward the house. He hopes she didn't notice.

He touches the phone in his pocket, like rubbing a security blanket. He has to call Todd. No way he can keep this up. He simply cannot fake calm for the whole weekend. Quickly he realizes he has to get away for a minute or two, can't risk any of the conversation with Todd being heard. The house isn't that big. He knows he has to make the call safely away from his family.

"I think I'm going to go on a walk," Davis calls out to Hattie. "Stretch my legs after the drive."

Hattie is almost to the front door but turns back toward him. "Now that sounds good. Let's unpack the car, get the girls settled in and we can take a little walk. By ourselves."

"I really want to just clear my head before I get to work," Davis says. "Get my thoughts together for the deck I need to work on."

He sees it on her face. She's feeling a quick jolt of rejection. Of course she does. She has no idea what's going on. He's never turned down the chance to spend a few childless moments with her. He told her they would get away, get out of town for a while, and now he's telling her to stay away from him. He can tell she's feeling a distance between them grow.

He feels it too, and he knows he's the one making it swell into something he might not be able to fix. He's letting his mistakes, his failures, create feelings of rejection and suspicion. He's the one allowing them to take root in the most important relationship in his life. Justin and LA are already driving them apart, and Davis is helping it happen.

"You know what?" Davis says. "Screw that. Let's go. Please, would you take a walk with me?"

Hattie smiles big.

"Okay," she says, "but coffee after, right?"

"Absolutely."

24

____

Davis's mind twists pretzel-like, wrapping into tight coils of worry while he thinks back to the walk with Hattie.

As he drives to the store, a fresh hit of self-hate spikes inside of him. A new gut-punch of guilt, regret and disbelief robs him of the clear mind he so desperately seeks. A mindset he hasn't enjoyed of late. There's a vibration of anxiety that's been present ever since he left LA. A layer of anxiety that he didn't even realize was there until he and his wife started their walk together. He thought it had left him, at least taken a break, but the anxiety came back like a bad penny.

For a bit, during the drive, he felt like himself. Like normal. Briefly, there was a flicker of normalcy. That walk, what should have been a nice memory for them, was now cold.

They talked. Well, she talked. He was distant, trapped in his new faraway place. Davis was there physically, right beside her, but a million miles away at the same time. His mind was with people like Todd, Justin, Tilley. Not even remotely present, not even on the same planet as Hattie.

She held his hand. He barely squeezed it, letting it hang like a loose glove.

She was sweet, kind, loving. He was a walking shell of her husband.

She probably feels more rejected than before, he thinks. Everything he does is a mistake. Every instinct is wrong. Davis feels himself slipping away, with no idea of how to stop it all from sliding into nothing.

This is why he's in the car again. He's driving to the store on a bullshit trip to get coffee. There was plenty in the house—two fresh, unopened bags —but Davis got to the pantry before Hattie could see it. He buried the coffee, both bags, in the trash cans outside after they got back from the walk while she went to the bathroom.

He pretended he didn't hear her cry as he slipped back into the house. It was soft, restrained, but he knows the sound. He hates that sound.

When she got out, Davis told her there wasn't any coffee in the house and that he needed to run to the store down the road. After the emptiness of the walk, Hattie didn't even bother to question it or offer to come along. What was the point?

She did say, half-heartedly, with eyes puffy and red? Something about him not needing to do that. Davis quickly said that it would give him some time to clear his head, to think about the new slide deck. She didn't fight it. She didn't care about his reasons.

Not at all.

The guilt that was slowly taking up residence inside of Davis has become a permanent fixture now. A tenant that might never leave. Before LA it didn't exist. A day ago it burned into him upon entry. It wriggled and itched. Now, this guilt is a part of him, like a tumor that cannot be removed. Something that resides inside him, along with any other emotion or vital organ. He's becoming comfortable with it. Becoming friendly with it. Making friends with guilt.

My new buddy. A tumor named Justin.

He smirks, thinking that would make a great self-help group introduction, but knows there's nothing funny about what he's becoming. He can feel the seismic shift in his head. Thoughts he'd never entertain in the past are now becoming way too common for him, far too easy to form. Worse, too easy to reconcile, to compartmentalize. The lies. The sectioning off of it all. All of it placed carefully into tiny boxes and shoved into a closet of wrong that he keeps locked in the back of his mind. That closet is bursting at the hinges, however. The knob is turning, and what's in there wants to come out.

And it's in no mood for play.

Davis grips the wheel tight. This has to end. There needs to be a refresh, a rewind. A way of getting back to good. A cleansing of this guilt-based relationship he's taken on with his family. One that was once built on much more than that. There has to be a reset button with Hattie. He wants to go back so badly, to roll things back to a few days ago.

"Back to good," he whispers to himself.

Memories of leaving for the airport to head to LA creep in. The girls were sad, their tiny arms offering tight hugs squeezing around his neck. Then they'd slide down and cling to his legs, barely letting him walk to the door. Hattie gave him a nice hug with a sweet kiss as well. The look in her eyes then was filled with something Davis can't define. It's much, much different than the look he received when he left her a few minutes ago to head to the store.

She used to look at him with love, with affection, with trust. It was standard. No action necessary. No fee to pay.

Will that look come back? Can it ever return after all of this?

Davis knows damn well there's only one way to

get it back. He has to earn it. There's a plan in motion. He's got to follow through with the plan he and his friend started. It has to work. Pulling his phone from his pocket, he dials up Todd.

"You at the lake?" Todd barely gets out before Davis jumps in.

"What's going on with the detective?"

"You gotta chill out, man. There are a lot of people looking into a lot of things."

"What *things*?"

"Davis—"

"Todd, goddamn it. Tell me what the hell is going on!" Davis realizes he is screaming. His face is hot, the hairs on his arms standing straight up. He's gripping the steering wheel so hard his knuckles are white, and he can barely feel the wheel in his fingers.

There's a deafening silence. Only the sound of the tires gripping the road.

After what seems like hours, Todd finally speaks.

"Look, I'm glad you are all safe at the lake house, and I know this isn't easy, but you need to just hang out and do nothing."

"Is that a joke?"

"I've got people digging into this Justin prick. They're tracing the charges he made to the cards. We're firing out calls, emails, texts. We're out all over the place."

"And?"

Davis hears Todd sigh, can feel his friend collecting his thoughts even over the phone.

"They can't find anything about this guy's company. This JR FUN INC," Todd says. "They can't find anything about who he even is."

Davis feels himself float. His brain sloshes inside his head, unable to hold onto a clear, stable thought. It's almost as if he's watching himself from above, watching himself come apart at the seams and then sink into the ground. He's become an audience member looking on, watching the show, soaking in the destruction of Davis Briggs.

He tries to speak, his lips move, but nothing comes out.

"What?" Todd asks.

"What do I do?"

"We'll get this guy. Only a matter of time. No one is a complete ghost. Not in today's world. There has to be a footprint of this asshole somewhere."

"I should just pay him."

"With what?"

"I could—"

"You don't have any money, man."

"I can figure something out. Equity from the house, maybe. The girls' college plans."

"Do you hear yourself?"

Davis's eyes are on the road, but the images

barely graze the inside of his head. He's on autopilot, lucky that he knows his way around this area, otherwise he'd be lost in more ways than one.

He pulls the car into a small grocery store parking lot in a space toward the front. After sliding it into park he slumps back, pushing himself as deep into the seat as he can. He presses the phone hard to his ear, as if that will help make the conversation between him and Todd better. Make it clearer. Easier to accept, to understand.

"Then tell me," Davis says. "What the hell should I do?"

"Like I said, do nothing. It's the easiest and the hardest thing in the world to do right now. Give me the rest of the week."

"He keeps calling. He keeps slamming me with texts. I'm going to have to find a way to pacify this guy."

"You don't think you can just ignore the asshole?"

"He's just getting more and more pissed off. I'm afraid he'll come looking for me, and eventually he will find me. You don't know this guy. He's a different kind of animal." Davis pauses. "I can't have that, Todd. Not with Hattie and girls."

"That's not going to happen."

"How do you know?"

"We're not going to let it."

Davis watches a mother push a cart with her

baby sitting in the front. The child's face is bright with eyes stuffed with wonder. The mother tickles the baby's belly, smiling and laughing along with her child. The baby giggles and bobbles its head without a care in the world. A perfect blank slate, only needing to be loved and shown the world by people who care. He thinks of the girls when they were that way. God he misses it. He thinks of them now, of how they need him more now. They need to be protected by those same loving and caring people from when they were babies. He's possibly put them in harm's way. He's broken his unwritten contract with them. His heart jumps to his throat merely off the thought.

"A week is a long damn time. A lot can go wrong in a week."

"I know." Todd thinks, then says, "Okay, how about this? Tell Justin that you don't have any more money. Literally. You can't pay him."

"Already did."

"Convince him. Go next level. Cut off contact."

"He'll freak the hell out. This guy's not stable. He'll go crazy."

"Tell him you're bankrupt after all those charges."

Something in Todd's statement rings true to Davis. He lets the word *bankrupt* turn over in his head.

"I don't have any money after putting it all into the business." Davis talks while he thinks, using his spoken words to string together his thoughts. "I never had any to begin with, I just wanted people to think I did."

"Yeah," Todd says, not sure what Davis is doing here. "I guess so."

Davis lets the idea swirl, taking laps around his clouded mind. He knows that will make for an uncomfortable-as-hell conversation, to say the least, but it will buy them some time. Time for Todd's people to find something useful or, better still, find a way out of this. That's all Davis can do right now. Buy time.

"Maybe," Davis says more to himself, "I'll tell him that. He can't squeeze blood from a stone. More I think about it, you're so right. He will freak out, but let him. Maybe I'll give it a day, if I can. The more time we can stall the better." Davis nods to himself, taking a second to think. "Okay. I'll do it. I'll try."

"Okay, man. You know best," Todd says. "Try not to stress too much. I'm on it."

"Thanks, man. I know you've done a lot—"

"Don't thank me yet."

Davis smiles as he hangs up, taking a minute to get ahold of himself. He knows Todd isn't much for sentimentality, and stopped Davis before he could properly say "thank you."

Checking his face in the rearview mirror, Davis sees his eyes are puffy and red. Much like Hattie's when he left. His skin is blotchy, as if he's been crying for days. He has, in a way. The stress has gone to work on him. He might not have been crying actual tears, but his mind has been processing sadness all the same. Perhaps the body doesn't know the difference, processing sorrow the same way, no matter how you express it.

Slapping his cheeks, he tries to snap out of it.

Todd will do everything he can to make this right. Davis knows Todd feels somewhat responsible too. He'll never admit it, but he knows Todd, and he knows that Todd feels guilty for sending Davis out to LA in the first place. Todd has busted Davis's balls about being married with kids for a long time. Todd lives like a trust fund baby frat boy, and he is all that to some degree, but he loves what Davis has and the family he's built.

Over drinks, many drinks, Todd has confessed that he wants a family. Wants someone to come home to. Someone he cares about, and someone who cares for him, regardless of income. It was the only time Todd has ever truly left himself wide open to Davis. It was the rawest form of Todd that Davis has ever seen. The next day he tried to talk more about it with Todd. Todd acted like he had no idea what Davis was talking about. Told him to stop projecting his married misery on him and went on a rant about how married zombies are always trying to force their shit on single people.

It's also not lost on Davis that Todd has more selfish, business-oriented reasons to get this Justin situation resolved. The Justin problem, as Todd previously stated, can quickly become a business problem, and that's a problem that greatly affects Todd. If you bundle all that together—the business, Todd's feelings about Davis and his family—then it's pretty clear Todd will stop at nothing to help Davis fix all of this.

A true alignment of interests.

Davis turns up the radio. "Blue Skies" by Willie Nelson plays. He loves Willie, and much like he did with the Pixies song, he tries to let the music calm him down. Take him to another place.

His phone buzzes. There's a new text from Justin.

hey i know ur not a txt guy so i'm moving on to email. got this great app with a delay. so the email i just sent to you will go out to all your contacts in like 24 hrs from now. just fyi. lemme know if you want me to stop it.

Davis fumbles, tapping and swiping fingers to move over to email on his phone. There's a single red number one. A single unread message from JR FUN INC. He taps it fast.

There are no words in the email. No explanation. No threats. Only images.

A lot of them.

A gallery of dirty deeds, all with Davis as the star.

Some of them he's seen, others he wishes he didn't. It's an ocean of depravity that no man with a family wants to see his face being a part of. It's an avalanche of colors and shapes. Bodies. Flesh pressed together. Mouths pressed together. Smiles. Laughing. Tongues licking. Teeth biting. Faces frozen in pleasure. Others in pain. Women Davis doesn't remember. Skin stretched tight over muscles slick with oil.

Two are even more graphic images.

Pictures of Davis penetrating deep inside a now familiar woman. The green-eyed beauty from the grocery store. Her mouth is open. Her eyes closed.

Davis focuses on his own eyes. They seem crazed. Fixed pupils looking like bullet holes. Focused and distant at the same time. He knows it's him, but it's not him at all. More like a copy of him, living a separate life he has no knowledge of.

Scrolling down the email he finds one more picture.

The pictures seem to have been placed carefully in an order. An order designed to escalate in intensity. Each one a little worse. Each one a little more embarrassing. Each one becoming harder and harder to look at. But the last one, this is the one

Justin has been holding on to, all of these images building to a finale.

It's of Tilley.

She's lying on the floor of Davis's hotel room in LA.

Her throat is cut wide open, blood having poured out onto the carpet.

Davis drops his phone onto the floorboard of the car. The picture matches the flickers of memory that have been popping in and out of his head. She was alive in his memories, at least he thought so, but now he knows different.

Is that what Justin was talking about in that parking lot?

Did I kill her?

"No," Davis says out loud, then screams, "No!'

He rolls down the window letting some air in. His stomach twists and turns as he sucks in deep breaths, fighting back the urge to throw up. It's as if every ounce of blood in his body has raced to his head. The pounding is unbearable. Can't feel his hands or his legs. His face feels like it's pressed against a frying pan. His eyes are wide open, but see nothing.

Davis knows he has to look at his phone again, but he never wants to see those images ever again.

They can't be real.

He rubs his hands together, shaking them hard while trying to gain control over the trembling. It's not working. Picking up his phone from the floor, he goes back over to the last text from Justin. His heart freezes as he rereads the words over and over again.

so the email I just sent...

will go out to all your contacts in like 24 hours...

lemme know if you want me to stop it.

25

His brain has been set ablaze.

His body quivers in sudden, intense bursts. His guts dive down hard as he turns one question over and over again: is this the end? Is this the end of everything he loves? A single, paralyzing thought that nothing will ever be okay again. If Hattie sees those pictures, that's it. Game over. She'll leave, and who could blame her? She'll take the girls and there'll be nothing Davis can do about it. If those pictures get out to all of his contacts, to all of his business contacts, to all of his friends and family, he'll never be able to look anyone in the eye again. No one will speak to him. They will distance themselves from him completely. No one will give him safe harbor.

Not even Todd.

The company will be lost or, at the very least,

Davis's part will be. Davis hasn't even begun to consider the legal problems if the police see those pictures. Tilley has to have been reported missing by now.

Justin has just been playing with him before now. Toying with Davis like a dog with a tiny bug. Justin was on the fringes of breaking Davis's life in half in the beginning, but the mood has changed. Now Justin pressed a button, went nuclear, and blasted Davis's existence to smithereens.

Davis rocks back and forth in the seat with his face wrapped in his hands. The sight of those pictures has burned into his head. He doesn't remember them being taken. Doesn't remember being in any of those situations. With any of those people. Any of it. How can the brain erase things like that? Gloss over everything that happened in those pictures? Davis knows he was drugged, but that can't explain everything, can it?

Can it explain away all the sexual acts with those people?

Can it grant forgiveness?

The last picture has shaken Davis to the core. The picture at the bottom of the email is cemented in his head, and is not going anywhere. The one of Tilley. Her throat cut wide open. Her blood so dark, spilled out into the carpet. Her lifeless eyes staring up toward the sky, perhaps looking up to

Davis's. Looking to him for answers. Asking why, why did he do this to her?

How could I not remember that?

How is that even possible?

Looking out the car window, he sees a man walking toward the front door of the store. Something about him is familiar. The profile. The walk.

Is that Justin?

"What the hell?" Davis whispers.

Davis can't completely make out the features, but it could be him. He's dressed different. There's no slick suit. This guy's in a flannel shirt and dirty jeans with a beanie over his head, but it could be him. There's something so damn familiar about him. Davis shakes his head, trying hard to clear the fog. He squeezes his burning eyes closed, then opens them, working fast, blinking hard to try and get a better look.

The man opens the door with a slight bow, letting a mother and baby exit the store. The same mother and baby Davis saw earlier. The man smiles and waves to the baby. Davis now sees that the man has a large scar, maybe a birthmark, on the side of his face and is missing a few teeth. It's not Justin. Not even close.

I'm losing it.

He can feel paranoia wrapping around him like an unwanted hug from a stranger. Fingers digging into his back, squeezing hard, robbing him of his

ability to breathe. Davis's eyes dance around the
parking lot, scanning for Justin, knowing that he's
there watching him... but not knowing for sure.
He's being careful, he tells himself. He knows deep
down inside that the odds of Justin finding him out
here are remote, but Justin is playing a different
game.

A different kind of animal, like he told Todd.

Davis is playing checkers while Justin plays
chess.

His phone buzzes. Davis almost throws it out
the window.

It's a text from Hattie.

U still at the store?

Davis realizes he's been gone awhile. Time has
gotten away from him. He has no idea when he left
the house. He's even forgotten why he's here in the
first place. His mind is mush, a useless mass taking
up space inside of his skull. He thinks, knows he
needs to get inside the store and get something.

What? Think.

Straining the back corners of broken memories,
he struggles to remember why in the hell he came
here.

"Coffee. Shit," he says to himself.

Davis answers the text by telling Hattie yet
another lie. A lie about how there's a long line and
it's crazy-busy for some reason. The last thing
Davis needs right now is coffee, his heart is a steady

redline, but he knows he needs to get in that store and get out quick or Hattie's suspicion will rise higher than it probably already has.

Come on, Todd. I'm going down fast. Do something.

Davis hurries through the aisles, hunting for coffee in an unfamiliar store. The rows and rows of colorful packaging blur. Hard to focus, difficult to stop the swirling thoughts whipping through his bending mind. He grabs a bag of some kind of coffee that looks decent and spots the refrigerated section down a few aisles. Maybe picking up Hattie's favorite chocolate and peanut butter combo trick would be a good idea.

A peace offering. Something to soothe the wounds.

Knowing what he knows it sounds ridiculous, pathetic even, but he's willing to try anything. Ice cream smoothing over a night of wholesale infidelity and murder? Davis laughs out loud. An older man looks at him strangely. Davis shrugs and continues snickering as he walks toward the front.

As he nears the cashier, he stops cold.

The cashier looks a lot like Justin.

He knows he was being paranoid with the guy outside, but this one, this guy looks even more like Justin. Davis avoids eye contact as he inches up in the line, making his way toward the front of the check out. Stealing glances at the cashier, Davis snaps a series of pictures of the man's face in his mind then turns them over, flipping them in his head, taking in all the angles.

His hair is different. Eyes might be a bit wider, maybe narrower, but those both can be altered rather easily.

It can't be him. Right?

The nose looks off too, but again, that can be changed.

Is he using makeup?

Davis moves closer and closer. Only a younger man with coupons stands between him and the cashier. Davis feels his heart pound in his chest. His breathing quickens. His instinct for flight is surging inside of him.

"Hey there, friend."

Davis looks up, panic firing.

The cashier's face scrunches up off of Davis's terrified expression. "You okay, friend?"

"I'm... fine. Sorry," Davis says while studying the cashier's face, still unsure of whom he's talking to. "Just these, please."

Davis sets the coffee and ice cream on the counter, letting the cashier scan them, never taking his eyes off of him.

"Alrighty then," the cashier says with a chirp.

Davis can't help but notice there's a strangeness to this guy. He bounces on his heels, almost dancing behind the counter. Like he's living in his own rhythm. He talks to himself as he scans the ice cream. Not singing a song, but whispering something to himself, maybe even reciting something.

"Excuse me?" Davis says. "Did you ask me something?"

The cashier shakes his head with a fast jerk like he's resetting his head.

"Nothing," he says to Davis. "I drift a little bit at times. Sorry, friend. In my own little world, I guess."

Davis nods. The cashier goes back to his task.

"Bet you'll be the hero."

"What?" Davis asks, his tone sharper than he intended.

"This." The cashier holds up the ice cream. "Bet the house beasts will love the stuffing out of you for this stuff."

"House beasts?"

"Your kids," the cashier says, cocking his head. "You've got 'em, right? Kids? Children? House beasts?"

Davis feels bumps rise up along his arms. This guy, this cashier, who is he?

"How do you know if I have kids?"

"I don't. Simply a guess, I suppose. It's cool if you don't. I like ice cream, too."

The cashier goes back to his task, whistles some uneven tune, then bags up Davis's coffee and ice cream.

Davis looks him over again. He's becoming less and less like Justin. This guy is goofy. Strange, awkward. Very different from Justin. More of a quirky local guy than anything resembling Justin. The way he talks is not at all like Justin, but there's something about him that still has Davis questioning everything.

Davis drops some cash on the counter, then grabs the bag from the cashier's hand.

"That's too much, friend."

"Keep it," Davis says, exiting the store as fast as he can.

"We don't take any tips. Policy."

Davis races to find the safety of his car. Dropping the bag into the passenger seat, he starts the car, letting himself breathe again. The air conditioning hits his face. He loves the way it cools the heat off his face. He tries to get ahold of his bouncing emotions. He feels like he's coming undone. The velocity of his fall is increasing, multiplying by the second.

He slams his hands on the steering wheel again and again, harder and harder, to the point he only feels a slight tingle in his hands as they slap the leather over and over again. The dash rattles and jumps. The change in the cup holder dances. He watches the palms of his hands pound the wheel, almost marveling at how hard he can hit the thing without feeling anything. Only faint pressure, but that's even becoming more and more faint. He wishes he could do that with the rest of him.

To his mind. To his emotions.

Get to where he feels nothing.

He stops slapping the wheel. His hands tingle. His lungs are heavy like he's been running hard sprints. He wants to cry. Wants to give in, to unload these feelings that are dragging him down. The desire for it all to stop is overwhelming. He stares out the window, watching the people come and go, but seeing nothing at the same time. They barely register as humans, perhaps not human at all. They're all only things to him right now. Faceless blobs in motion.

He's losing his grip on things, that much is clear.

He's slipping away.

If he isn't already gone.

26

Davis walks into the lake house.

He sat out in the car for several minutes getting himself together, knowing that he looked like hell, before psyching himself up to come inside. Knowing that his emotions were bubbling near the edge, he did his best to calm himself in the car, practiced smiling into the mirror. Faking that everything is okay. He worked through a few lines and a laugh to keep in his back pocket.

Hattie is playing a board game on the floor with the girls. She glances up, barely acknowledging he's there.

The dog jumps on his legs.

Davis knows she's off, that she's not over the walk. She's not back to good. Not vaguely close. He didn't expect a miracle while he was gone, but he hoped for the best. There's a vacancy in the way

she moves her piece around the board. A lifeless-
ness to how she's playing with their daughters. He's
never seen this before, never seen her so removed.

His mind is still fumbling with thoughts of the
cashier at the store. On the drive back he convinced
himself it wasn't Justin, then convinced himself it
was, then not again. Now he's landed at not being
completely sure. It's safer to be suspicious than
completely dismiss the idea it was him. It's the
smarter way to play this.

It could have been him.

It can't be.

Was it him?

The girls giggle, finally, and so does Hattie. She
looks over to her husband, getting a real look at him
for the first time since he's been back. He's still a
mess, despite his best efforts. His eyes are still red.
His face hangs from his skull like a wet towel over a
rack.

"You okay?" she asks.

Davis is lost in his own mind. Picking at the
edges for answers. There are none to be found.

"Sweetheart?"

*His nose was different, but something about his
voice sounded familiar.*

"Hello?"

*Those pictures. Oh God, the pictures. Is Tilley
really dead? Did I—*

"Davis!"

He jumps, stumbles back, then turns to Hattie as he's shaken free from his trance. Forced out of his head and into the real world. The girls laugh then begin to roll on the floor, thinking the expression on Daddy's face is funny. He looks like he was suddenly awoken from a nightmare—eyes wide, face frozen.

"What's wrong? Did something happen at the store?" Hattie asks.

"No." Davis scrambles to find cover. "I was working through a presentation in my head on the way back. Sorry, I got lost for a second."

Hattie gets up, not really buying it, but not wanting to dig into whatever is going on between them in front of the girls.

"Did you get coffee?"

"Yeah, yes. Here. And..." He shows her the ice cream like it was some lost artifact never seen by civilized eyes.

"Oh," Hattie says. "Thanks. That's nice."

She takes the coffee and ice cream and heads to the kitchen. Her walk and expression are void of her normal energy for life. Davis's strange behavior is starting to wear her down. He can see it, too obvious to ignore now, but he has no idea what to do about it. Solutions fail him. The pictures on his phone burn through his head like a horrific slide show, one after another, tearing away at him.

He looks to his girls.

They play, then fight, then play. Not a care in the world, only mild flashes of drama that fade away as quickly as they started. Both of them wrapped up in a feeling of safety. Safety forged by trust and love, both of which Davis has put into jeopardy. He has betrayed their trust.

He thinks of the cashier.

Davis heads into the kitchen. He leans against the counter while Hattie fills the coffee maker with water while avoiding eye contact. No hint at wanting conversation.

He thinks of the cashier. Of the things he said. They felt knowing. Personal.

"Did you tell anyone we were coming here?" His words are biting, accusatory. He didn't mean them to be, but he's losing the ability to control the way he communicates. Words are merely a tool for getting answers, now.

"What?"

"Did you tell what's-her-name down the street or post anything anywhere?"

"No," she says, turning toward him. She's clearly not happy with his tone. "You said you wanted to get away. Just us. You wanted privacy. Said you wanted to get some things done and, oh yeah, spend time with your family."

Davis looks down. That's what he said. His own words weaponized against him.

"Am I missing anything?" she says, holding her

stare. "Now you're doing what? Accusing me of a security leak?"

"No, I—"

"What is going on with you, Davis?" She softens, her eyes filled with concern and confusion. "Talk to me. Something is clearly wrong."

Davis can see it all over her face. It's in her voice. She's worried. She cares about him, about them, and wants to help, but she doesn't understand.

How could she?

Davis doesn't understand any of this either. He's wandered into a place that he never intended to visit. A wrong turn, a misstep, led him, led them, to a bad spot. One he's not sure he can navigate. One he could really use her help with—*Hattie the Great would know what to do*—but he knows he has to do this without her.

She has no idea what's wrong, and Davis hopes she never will.

"I'm sorry," he says.

"Just tell me what is happening. Let me help. I'm a pretty smart kid."

Davis cracks a smile. It feels nice. "It's not that."

"What. Is. It?"

Davis gets lost in her eyes. Eyes he's known for so long.

He remembers something they set up between them long ago. They developed a signal between them they used mostly at parties or bars. A wordless, subtle signal to let the other know something needed to be done. Usually meaning that one of them was trapped in a conversation they wanted desperately to get out of. Sometimes it was used when one of the girls was out of control and they needed some help fast. One time, Davis was fumbling with fixing the fence and gave her the signal from across the yard. It was simple: make eye contact and then bite their lower lip. That was it. They've used time and time again and it's saved both of them over the years.

As he looks into her eyes, he wants so badly to be back at a party with her. To go back to those days.

They've been through a lot together. Good times and bad. They survived the pitfalls of most marriages, lasted longer than a lot of their friends. Davis knows this situation, this Justin situation, is like nothing they've been through before, however. This isn't anything like the feeling of being buried alive in money problems. It's not going nights without sleep, worrying about food and shelter while your babies sleep next to you. It's not the helpless feeling of not being able to cover your bills no matter how hard you stretch.

This is far worse.

This is a different kind of animal.

And it's threatening to tear them apart.

"Tell me," Hattie begs.

The pictures in Justin's email sear, burning him down from the inside out.

"I'm really tired," he says, his eyes filling. "That's all."

She bites her lip. Only now it's completely different than when they were younger. She's completely defeated, knowing there's something important he's not telling her. He was close, maybe, to telling her, to letting her in. They were so close to cracking this wide open, together, but he recoiled back into his secure place, retreated deep into his own emotional quarantine, walling her off once again.

She turns away, focusing again on the coffee.

"It's the business," he tries. "There's a lot of stress, that's all."

"Okay."

"Really, that's it. I'm sorry—"

"It's fine. I'll make some coffee. Go check on the girls."

Davis sees that things are anything but *fine*, but he also knows when to stand down. He slips out from the kitchen and heads back into the living room. He stands a few feet away, watching the girls. They continue to laugh and fight, then fight and laugh. What normally would be a wonderful moment watching his children is anything but that.

His shoulders rise up toward his ears. A tension spike reaches up to his head. As he rubs his temples, he notices the blinds are wide open, giving a full view of the living room from the outside. Davis rushes over, shutting them fast. He checks the locks on the front door two, then three times. Scanning the room, he starts making quick calculations of entry and exit points. He's going through a worst-case scenario planning exercise in milliseconds.

He hears Hattie finishing up in the kitchen. He'll check the back later.

Needing to check in with his email and with Todd, Davis decides to head to his makeshift office. As he passes his girls, he pats them each on the head as he slips into the small bedroom he'll use as his office.

Opening up his laptop, he lets it whiz and whirl as it boots up its digital brain. While he waits he closes his eyes, trying to recharge. To reshuffle his mental deck. Hoping a quiet alone moment will give him some sense of calm.

It does not.

The second he shuts his eyes the images scream through his mind once again. The pictures. Justin. The women. Tilley with her throat almost ripped out.

He squeezes his eyes tighter, shifting gears in his head now, replaying his last few conversations with Hattie. Each one was an escalation. Every word displaying her diminishing trust. Her eyes questioning her husband more and more. He allows himself a moment to imagine her leaving him, her walking out with the girls. The simple act of thinking about his family leaving him causes his throat to close, inducing a hard cough to fire from his lips.

Her packing.

Him pleading.

The girls crying.

Tilley with her throat cut.

"Hey."

Davis spins around in his chair toward the door. Hattie stands in the doorway, barely making eye contact as she hands him a cup of coffee. It's the perfect shade of caramel, just enough cream, the way they've always had their coffee.

"I just realized I need a couple of things for dinner," she says. "Sorry, should've had you pick them up while you were out."

Davis freezes, thinking of the cashier. He starts to get up, grabbing his keys. She puts up a hand. "No, I'll go, you just got back. Get some work done. The girls want to get out for a second anyway."

Davis can't let them go to that store. Not while

there's even the vaguest possibility Justin might be there. He knows it's not him. But it might be.

"I should go."

"Don't be ridiculous." She motions to the computer. "Do whatever you need to do and come back to us."

Davis looks to her, lost. Her words hit hard, even if she didn't intend them to. Her expression hits even harder.

"Okay?" she asks.

He nods. "Please go to a different store. Not the one at the bottom of the hill. Go to the one farther in town."

"Why? That's like fifteen minutes farther out."

Davis scrambles. "The one I went to was a mess. Remodeling and stuff. The girls will drive you nuts there, trust me."

"Okay," she says, a hint of disbelief trailing in her voice as she leaves.

There's an undeniable coldness to her, as if she were talking to a stranger. Maybe Davis is imagining things, or being too sensitive to everything, but he feels the two of them are miles apart. It's in everything she's done since he got back from the store. Her speech. Her stance. That woman in the doorway just now looked like his wife in every way, but she seemed almost like a complete stranger.

A stranger in his own marriage.

Davis leans back in his chair, watching Hattie

gather up the girls and lead them out the door. Tears begin to well in his eyes like a hard rain that's been growing in intensity. The water levels are building up more and more with each passing moment, rising faster and faster.

And the dam is about to burst wide open.

27

AT DINNER that night there's an unmistakable emptiness.

The growing distance is palpable. Even the girls can sense it now. They aren't giggling or cutting up at the table as they usually do. They pick at their food, sitting quietly while stealing quick glances between them. Mostly looking down, but occasionally looking at their mom and dad. They're young, but they can see something is wrong between them. They can feel it.

Hattie smiles forced smiles back at them. Davis does the same. Damage control. The girls give half-smiles in return then look down, pushing food around their plates with limited interest in eating it.

The only sound at the table is the occasional clicking of forks and spoons. Davis can't remember a night at the dinner table that was this quiet. No chatter about the day. No laughter. No joy. Not even the hum of sisters bickering. He wants to tell them to start talking, wants them to make some kind of sound.

He wants to scream out, *Say something!*

He doesn't.

He cuts another chunk of chicken and chews in silence. The air in the house seems to have become thick. Tight.

Hard to breathe in here, he thinks while rubbing his throat.

Davis considers checking the thermostat, even though he knows that's insane. The temperature out here by the lake drops at night. His face feels hot again. Flush. He tugs at his T-shirt collar. His palms have a wet coldness to them that's been coming on since the store. Setting down his fork, he rubs his thumbs into the palms of his hands, trying to solve the problem he's ignored since this afternoon. He notices Hattie stealing a glance at him. Davis quickly picks up his fork, returning to his chicken.

Hattie clears her throat, breaking the silence. "I forgot," she says. "I ran into someone who said they knew you."

Davis drops his fork onto his plate. The clang makes the girls jump in their seats.

"What?" Davis says.

"A guy at the store said he knew you. Nice guy. A little off, but nice."

"What did he say?"

"He said he's known you for a while—"

"He what? Listen, this is important. What exactly did he say?" Davis's questions are hard. Biting. His heart pulsing up into his throat. "What did he look like?"

"He was—"

He grabs her hand, squeezing it way too tight.

"Tell me everything, Hattie. What did he do?"

Hattie rips her hand back, looking at him like he's lost his mind.

"What's wrong with you?"

"What did he look like?"

"Davis, what—"

"Was he dumb and goofy or was he slick and good-looking? Cool? Hip guy, wearing nice clothes?"

The girls look to each other, not liking what's going on. One of the girls' eyes begins to water. The other is getting mad. One mad, the other sad at whatever is happening to their daddy.

"What is this? Are you, what, jealous?" Hattie says. "You think I'm picking up guys at the lake house store?"

"No. Hattie—"

"What is going on with you?"

"Nothing. Just tell me what the hell happened at the—"

"I can't even—"

Davis slams his fists down on the table. The plates and glasses jump.

"What the fuck happened?" he screams.

The room goes silent.

An old clock ticks in the living room.

It's as if all the energy had been sucked out of the house in the blink of an eye. Davis looks around the table. His wife and daughters look back at him like he's a complete stranger. Someone other than the man they know is sitting at the table with them. As if he's some crazy homeless man swinging at invisible people on the street. Someone they want to get away from. Someone they need to fear.

Seeing the look in his daughters' eyes stops Davis cold. It's a look he's never seen from them before. A look he's never seen from anyone. They're afraid. Afraid of him. He's been angry in front of them before, sure, but not like this, and never like this with their mother.

Something snaps inside of him. He wants to get up and hug them. Tell them he's sorry. Explain that everything is okay.

Except he knows that's not true.

He wonders if anything will ever be okay again.

"Come on," Hattie says to the girls. "Get your plates. We're eating in the bedroom."

"Why?" the girls ask.

"Daddy needs some alone time."

She gathers up her daughters, helping them pick up their plates and glasses, leaving her own behind on the table. Her food barely touched. They move off to the back bedroom, away from Davis, without looking back. Davis feels his chest rise and fall as he fights to get his breathing right. As the bedroom door shuts, he pushes away from the table hard, wanting to turn the table over and shatter everything on it to the floor.

He hates himself for what just happened, for how he handled it.

He has no idea how to smooth this over. This is something that will hang over them for a long time. Maybe forever. This is a memory the girls will hang on to their whole lives, and it cannot be undone. The night at the lake house when Daddy lost it at dinner because Mommy talked to a man.

A man.

Davis's guts churn, thinking that Justin is near. He's out there somewhere, roaming free. Was he really the cashier or did he pop up and introduce himself? Davis still doesn't know.

Did that monster talk to my family? Was it some kind of warning? That he can get to me anywhere?

His phone buzzes in his pocket. Davis jumps in his seat. A new chill rolls up his back. He releases a sigh of relief as he checks his phone. It's a text, but not from Justin.

This one's from Todd.

Talked to some people. Got some good ideas for getting rid of that asshole.

28

———

DAVIS WAKES up early the next morning.

He didn't sleep much. Short micro-naps in between checking his phone.

Hattie didn't come to bed last night.

He notices the door is still closed to the girls' room. He guesses she crashed in there for the night. Looking to her empty spot in the bed, he realizes something. This was the first night he and his wife hadn't slept in the same bed since they'd been married. They'd slept in the same bed many nights prior to getting married, of course, but last night was a first of sorts. At least, it's the first time it was a conscious decision to sleep separately. Davis doesn't travel much, so it's strange for Hattie not to be there when he wakes up.

He thinks of the last morning he woke up without her.

He thinks of LA.

His things neatly packed by the bed. His body freshly showered. His hair washed and combed. The hangover medicine laid out for him with the glass of water. The card on the dresser.

Davis gets out of bed and immediately heads to the small room he's turned into an office. Skipping coffee and food. He wants to dig into the emails Todd was supposed to send during the night. Todd's *good ideas for getting rid of that asshole.*

Davis tried to get ahold of him most of the night, but didn't hear back.

He fires up the computer, letting it work its magic. Looking back over the text from Todd last night, Davis feels a renewed hope this might still work out. Clinging to the edge of that hope, he lets his mind imagine a future day when this will all blow over.

Last night was a disaster, no doubt, but if Todd's right then Davis can still get past this little speed bump and return to the way life used to be. It'll take some time and a lot of work on his part, but he thinks he can get past it. The girls are young. Hattie might be a tougher sell.

As the computer finishes booting up, Davis starts up his email. He wants to jump out of his skin, waiting for the emails to load. All the notifications of *can't miss* sales, credit card deals and vacation getaway options stream down. There's only one sender Davis wants to see.

There it is.

Todd.

Davis opens up the email, scanning over what Todd sent only minutes ago. Most of it is Todd babbling about how amazing he is, per usual for Todd. The guy can't order a sandwich without throwing in some praise for himself. It used to rub him the wrong way, but Davis has come to love that about his friend. Part of him wishes he were more like that. More assertive in his own life. More confident in who he is. Davis marvels at how Todd charges through life as if he already knows the outcome is going to be a success.

Davis questions everything, as if he already knows the outcome is failure. This is also the thing that makes their partnership work. The balance between the two. There have also been more than a few times Davis has had to tap the brakes on one of Todd's tangents, a couple that could have broken the company.

Now Davis is the one about to break the company.

If those pictures get out, if their business contacts get a look at those, this business is over. Over before it really gets a chance to show what it can do. It kills Davis that he might be the architect of the company's demise. He loves what they've built, and the idea of being responsible for it crumbling continues to gnaw away at Davis's heart.

In the email, Todd says the lawyer and the investigator think they've got a line on who Justin is, but they still have some work to do. The investigator believes Justin is a shakedown artist who targets people in LA as mini cash cows. He's seen it before. They troll the fancy bars, hotels and restaurants to find a mark, then lock their jaws into the wealthy's throats and they will not let go. Davis was acting the part of "big-time tech startup money," and Justin went into attack mode. Jaws wide open. Fangs dug in.

Todd explained the nature of the pictures to the lawyer without going into too much detail, and the lawyer is pushing for Davis and Todd to protect themselves and the business. The lawyer's putting together some documents that might get rid of Justin, Todd's email says. Based on the idea Davis had, the thought is that if they show Davis has no money because of the business, then there's nothing for Justin to come after. Maybe they can pay Justin a smaller sum of cash, negotiate a buyout of sorts, so he feels like he's winning. If Justin believes that beyond that there's not more money to be had, then the hope is he'll take what he can get and slither away to someone else.

Davis lets the idea swirl around his head. For the first time in days he feels a sense of optimism. A feeling of progress. This is a plan that can work.

Davis steps out from the room, now needing a bite to eat and some much-needed coffee so he can process all the information in Todd's email. He's feeling human again. Basic needs coming back online. He's been so engrossed in his own thoughts that he hasn't noticed how quiet the house is. The door to the bedroom is open now. Davis peeks through the doorway. There's no sign of his family.

"Hello?" he says.

Nothing.

He sees some dishes in the sink and a pot of coffee on the burner. They've been up and obviously made and had some breakfast, but they're nowhere to be found.

"Hattie?" he calls out, growing more concerned. "Girls?"

The silence booms.

Davis opens the backdoor and steps outside into the yard. He hears voices. The girls are giggling, and he also hears Hattie laughing. Relief washes over him. He starts breathing again. One, he's glad they're there, and two, he's glad to hear their laughter again. The cold, hard tension from last night's dinner performance seems to have faded. At least that's what he tells himself. This is a hopeful sign that last night is in their rearview mirror. Maybe not completely, but it's a good sign.

As Davis turns the corner of the house, he sees his family standing on the pier that stretches out into the lake.

They are not alone. This stops him cold.

Slouched next to them is a man. Davis sucks in a hard gulp of air. It's the cashier. Davis's feet feel stuck in the ground. Planted. He can't move.

It's really him.

Only this time he's slightly less odd. He smiles and laughs with Hattie and girls. This guy seems more confident, more together than the guy working the register that Davis talked to yesterday. This guy is *more* in every way.

He's more Justin.

Davis wants to run down the pier, lower a shoulder and slam into him. Send him flying into the water then shove his head under until his lungs fill and this whole nightmare is over. He wants to feel his man's life end in his own hands.

The cashier cackles at a joke Hattie makes. Hattie snickers back. It's genuine, not polite or dismissive laughter to get through a conversation. Davis knows the difference. The girls run around the pier, laughing the whole time.

Davis feels the world tilt. The cashier turns to him. There's no question in Davis's mind now. That man is Justin. It's all in his eyes. The way he's looking at Davis, there is no mistaking it now. Justin gives the slightest of waves and places a soft hand on Hattie's back, pointing in Davis's direction. Hattie turns.

"Hey, honey." Her tone is mixed and guarded toward Davis, but still pleasant. "This is the guy I was talking about last night."

Davis's eyes zero in on Justin's hand still resting on his wife's back. Justin grins, slipping the hand slowly away from her, then gives Davis a finger-gun shot. Hattie moves down the pier toward her husband. Davis cuts the distance between them quickly, picking up his pace moving toward her. Davis never allows his stare to leave Justin.

Hattie is next to him now, but his children are still at the other end of the pier near the water, with Justin between him and the girls. Justin glances to them, then back to Davis, letting Davis know he can't do anything crazy without risking what Justin might do to them.

"He's funny. How do you know him?" Hattie says.

Davis places his hands on her shoulders. "Why don't you get the girls and go into town? See a movie or something."

"They're having fun outside."

"Please."

"Why?"

"Goddamn it, Hattie, listen to me. Just get them out of here, okay?"

Hattie steps back, disbelief riffling through her. She looks to her husband the same way she did last night when Davis lost it, when Davis the unwanted stranger came to the family dinner. Maybe she hoped it was a one-time appearance. Now she knows it's not. As her confusion fades, the anger begins to boil. She takes another step back.

"What the hell, Davis?"

"Hattie..." Davis keeps an eye on Justin, who rocks back on his heels without a care in the world. "I can't talk about it right now." He watches as Justin closes his eyes, letting the sun soak in while spreading his arms wide.

"Fine. I've tried. If you're not going to talk to me, then I... I don't know what to say."

Davis looks into his wife's eyes. He knows she's slipping away from him. He has to say something or risk losing her forever. He begins to say something, doesn't know what to say, then stops himself before a single syllable leaves his lips. She's taken aback by the look on his face. He looks broken. Lost. Davis knows he can't fool this woman or shield her from the truth, but in this case the truth will not help. It can only hurt.

"Hattie, you have to trust me," Davis says, on the verge of tears. "Please get the girls and go some-where. Anywhere. Away from the house."

Hattie stares at his face. Studying. Searching. Trying to read what's going on behind her husband's sad, broken eyes.

"Talk to me, please," Hattie says, begging for a connection with her husband. One she's never once thought she'd have to ask for.

Davis wants to tell her. Tell her everything right now, lay it all out for her here on this pier with Justin a few feet away. He desperately wants this all over, but he knows he can't tell her. He doesn't know how. The lies have piled up so high. An insurmountable wall that's bound to surround and close off his marriage, wall off a relationship with the love of his life.

"Hey, lovebirds," Justin says, stepping in. "Hate to interrupt, but I gotta bounce soon."

"We need to talk," Davis says to Justin. His tone is hard. Cold.

"Sounds serious." Justin's eyebrows fire up and he raises his hands, faking scared.

Hattie watches the two of them. Davis stands stiff, rigid, like his spine was made of steel. Justin, the cashier as she knows him, is bouncy. Playful. Almost like a puppy. Davis looks to his wife. He knows she doesn't understand, but he hopes she'll trust him enough to get the girls and get the hell out of there. He needs her to trust him.

One last time.

"Girls, we need to go," Hattie calls out, her eyes never leaving Davis. "I'll leave you to it."

"Bye, Hattie," Justin says.

Davis's teeth grind.

"Bye, Jerry," Hattie says. "Good to see you again."

Hattie gathers up the girls. They fight it briefly, but they can tell Mom isn't in the mood to play games. They move toward the house, away from the pier. Davis whips around to Justin, jamming his hands into Justin's chest with a hard jolt. He and Justin both are surprised by his sudden aggressive act. Felt good to Davis. Great even.

"Easy, Brutus," Justin says, laughing while rubbing his chest. "You should have seen your face when you walked up, man. Goddam priceless."

"What are you doing here?"

"Just hanging out, man."

"And this?" Davis flicks at the makeup on Justin's nose. "This shit?"

Justin's face shows a sign of being annoyed with Davis even trying to touch him. He slaps his hand away.

"I'm trying to have some fun. You remember fun, right?"

Davis stops cold.

"You remember what fun looks like?" Justin snaps his fingers, faking a light bulb going off in his mind. "Sure you do. You've seen the pictures."

Davis feels his heart begin to race again.

"How did you know I was here?"

"That is not the question you should be asking."

Davis moves closer, about to put hands on Justin again. Justin lands a sledgehammer of a punch to Davis's gut. All the air escapes from his lungs. Davis folds instantly. Justin puts a comforting hand on Davis's back, rubbing in large circles as if soothing a sick child.

"The question you need to ask is..." Justin singsongs, trying to coax an answer from Davis. "Come on now, you know. Just say it."

Davis coughs, fighting to find some air.

"I'll help ya out, okay? The question is now, and has always been, *how does Justin get his money?*"

Justin helps Davis stand up while looking around to make sure nobody saw that little sudden act of violence. He brushes off Davis's shoulders. Pinches his cheek.

"Now..." Justin holds his hand out. "Pay me."

"I don't have it."

"Pay me."

"I can't do that."

"It's pay me money, or we go to a plan B type of thing."

"What do you want from me?"

"Davis—"

"I don't have it," Davis says, thinking of the emails, his conversations with Todd. "I do not have any more money. Between the business and what I already paid you, it's all gone. Gone."

Justin steps back, taking a moment to look Davis over. To analyze him. Assess the man. He makes a finger-gun, clucks his tongue, then fires a shot at Davis. "Bullshit."

"I swear to God."

"God? Well, if you swear to God that's different."

"It's true. I've got nothing left."

"Prove it."

"I will." Davis swallows hard. "But you have to tell me something."

"Lay it on me."

"Why?"

"Why?" Justin looks around, scrunches his nose. "Why what?"

"Why all of this. Why are you tracking me down? The texts. The calls. The pictures. Disguising yourself at the store. All of it. Why?"

Justin moves in close. His eyes drill in. He softly kisses Davis on the forehead.

"Because I'm invested in you."

Davis's eyes pop wide as he pulls away from Justin.

"We're in this together, Big Fun." Justin smiles,

then removes a folded piece of paper from his pocket. He hands it to Davis's shaking hands.

"You go here tonight at, oh I don't know, midnight," Justin says with some flair. "Midnight sounds cool. Meet me there with your proof. If you're tapped out, you're tapped out. I can't get money from nothing, right?"

Davis nods, opening the paper. It's a map crudely drawn in crayon. Looks like a child's treasure map. The place appears to be on the other side of the lake, deeper into the woods. The meeting spot is marked with a fat, green smiley face.

"What proof do you need?" Davis says.

As he looks up from the paper, he realizes he's alone on the pier.

Justin is nowhere to be found. As if he vanished into thin air.

If it weren't for the paper in his hands, Davis would question if Justin was even there to begin with. Davis's fragile, broken mind is capable of just about anything right now. Imagining Justin playing with his wife and kids is not that much of stretch. Streaks of insanity have presented themselves slowly over the last few days. The fact that Justin was actually the cashier does provide Davis an odd bit of comfort, however. Maybe he's not completely cracking up.

Maybe he is.

He looks to the map. Meeting Justin in the

middle of the woods, in the middle of the night is last thing he wants to do. Every warning signal Davis has is telling him to tear up the map and run. Grab his family and run. Keep running until there's nowhere left to run.

He knows he can't.

He knows he has to be at this green smiley face at midnight.

He allows himself to let some hope seep back in. Amazed how quickly his mind can go from hope to catastrophe. He stares directly into the eyes of the fat, green smiley face. Not long ago he was convinced all was lost, then there was the possibility of things working out, then back to the sudden falling feeling of there being nothing he can do.

Davis realizes there is something he can do, however, and he needs to hold on to that idea. Hang on tight to the idea that he can always do something. A life void of hope is simply lost.

If Davis can prove to Justin that he doesn't have anything, no money to pay, that he's flat-out busted, then this could be all over. That was the plan he and Todd had been talking about. Davis can't believe he did it, but he got Justin to believe it was *his* idea. Davis worked the salesman's dream. The dream Todd described to him.

A thought swirls round and round, doing laps inside his head. A new confidence. A vulnerability has been found in Justin, a weak spot to strike in the armor. Davis can still win this and make things right. He'll have to move fast on it, but for the first time Davis knows he can make it work.

He's got something. A germ of an idea. An escalation in the plan.

He needs to talk to Todd.

29

"ARE YOU KIDDING ME?" Todd asks.

"It's going to work," Davis tells him, pressing the phone tight to his ear, talking low. He moves to shut the door to the bedroom. Before the door closes, he catches a quick look at his family sitting at the table having dinner. He told Hattie he wasn't hungry, that they should go on without him and he'd grab something later. Hattie didn't argue. Didn't say a word. Neither did the girls.

He's only pushing them further away while he's fighting like hell to keep them. Engineering the ever-widening space between him and his family. He hates it.

He hates all that's going on between them, but he's almost there. This is so close to being over. He can feel it. This whole ugly part of their lives is about to be done, if he can just drag himself across the finish line. There might be a growing distance between them, but if he doesn't do what he has to do right now, then his family could be lost for good.

"You want to sign everything away?" Todd asks.

"Have the lawyer draw it up. There's a transfer of ownership section in the contract."

"But, Davis—"

"It's above the 'transfer upon death' section." Davis is talking a mile a minute, letting his brain dump out into bursts of words. "He'll update the fifty-fifty ownership to a hundred percent to you. I'll do an e-signature on it, and that should be enough." He snaps his fingers, remembering something. "And have him backdate it. Make it a couple of days after LA."

"Not sure that's even vaguely legal."

"You can make him do it."

"Probably, but why?"

"It'll help the story. Also, have him draft a letter from you dated right after LA. Something about payment to me for the company. Make it for like twenty grand."

"But I didn't pay you—"

"It'll look like I was so busted I had to sell low to cover his bullshit, and now I have next to nothing. Not even the company." He pauses. Swallows hard. "Just an employee."

"And when it's over we make this all right, right? Get you back on the books, right?"

"Bet your ass."

"You sure about all this? I mean the lawyer can do it, but do you want this?"

"You got a better way?"

"No." Todd laughs. "I do, however, think you're out of your mind, and I love you for it."

"Control yourself," Davis says. "A wise man once told me, when you're all out of good ideas, you've got to go with the bad ones." Davis smiles, knowing he's echoing the words Todd told him when they started this thing.

There's silence on the other end of the phone. Davis knows he got to him. Todd's not one to show his feelings or, God forbid, talk about them, certainly not when he's sober, but he does have them. They come out in moments of silence. In pauses while he collects himself during an emotional moment. In a glossy-eyed look that gets covered quickly by a joke or a verbal jab.

The silence between them lingers. Davis knows this is one of those moments. He pictures Todd sitting wherever he is with his eyes red, filled with tears that will never fall.

"You there, boss?" Davis asks.

"Oh, I'm here," Todd says, his voice cracking. He coughs, then says, "Okay, I'll do it. I'll call the lawyer as soon as I get off the phone."

Davis pulls the map Justin gave him from his pocket, letting his eyes drift in and out of focus as his mind twists and bends. Playing out the possibilities of the future. Working through scenarios. Rolling toward what is going to happen out there in the woods beyond the lake at midnight.

What's waiting for me at that damn fat, green smiley face?

Only one way to find out.

"Last chance to back out," Todd says. "You're sure you want me to do this?"

Davis knows this is a decision he might not be able to fix later. There are an immeasurable number of things that can go wrong with this. He feels like he's standing at the edge of a diving board, high on top of a skyscraper, and one simple word spoken by him will be what pushes him off. Him giving that one simple word will send him hurtling down into the darkness of the abyss. A nosedive into the dark of the unknown, with no way to turn back.

Will there be a safe landing?

"Hey, you there? You sure you want me to do this?"

Davis licks his lips. Clears his throat.

He gives the one simple word.

"Yes."

PART IV

30

Davis's footfalls crunch the ground.

The barely legible map is clutched tight in his hand, while the moon provides his only light. He waited for Hattie and the girls to fall asleep before he slipped out of the house about an hour ago, lying awake in the shadows of the house, waiting for what seemed like forever. Waiting until he felt it was safe to go out into the night. He put on some clothes that could pass for exercise wear, just in case Hattie woke up and saw him, knowing damn well that wouldn't smooth the edges on any questions she'd have. Davis hasn't jogged in years, but it's better than no excuse at all.

No matter. This is all worth it. Peace is worth the risk. Peace for his battered brain. Peace for his home, for his children, for his wife, for what's left of his life. Davis's hope has been refreshed. Hope that this is the end.

His heart pumps hard against his ribs. He's not sure he's taken a breath since he left Hattie in bed, thankful she at least slept in the room tonight. He tried not to think about it, but as he looked to her his mind did wander to the idea that he might not be back. That this might be the last time he saw his wife. His children. So, he stole an extra second or two before he left, watching her sleep peacefully. He wanted to reach out. Touch her. Play with her hair like he used to. Tell her he loved her and that he was doing what he felt he had to do.

After he left the bedroom, he walked down the hall to the room their girls are sharing. Cracking the door open slightly, he stole a peek into the room. He didn't linger, not because he didn't want to, but because the pain of looking at his daughters was making him think of not leaving. His girls. The thought of never seeing them again was too much. He knew if he stayed much longer he might not leave at all. The longer he looked, the more he didn't want to go out into the night and meet Justin.

But Davis knew he had to come out here. Here in the woods, past the lake, under the midnight moonlight. Toward a spot on a map marked by a fat, green smiley face.

Davis readjusts his messenger bag that he has thrown over his shoulder. He opens it and checks the contents. He's checked five times since he left the house. Each time he does it he knows he's being completely paranoid, but he doesn't care. The importance of what's in this bag cannot be overestimated. This bag holds the future of everything. Everything that Davis has in the world.

He stops in his tracks, frozen, as if his feet have grown roots plunging deep into the ground. He hears the sounds of footsteps. Not running, but nothing creeping his way either. It's more the sound of feet dragging the ground, pausing, then stomping back down hard with a thump. A crackle of leaves. A brush of grass. The sounds are coming from up ahead, not far. Seems to be from over a slight hill that is just out of Davis's sight line.

He balls up his fists, feeling his nails dig into his palms. His heart rises up to the back of his throat. Breathing in deep, he releases the air from his lungs, then pushes himself to move up over the hill. The map tells him what's there—the fat, green smiley face tells him everything he needs to know.

As he clears the top of the hill, he can see Justin in a small open area surrounded by trees. As if nature has created a perfect circular stage, with trees as the audience.

Justin dances under the moon. Some form of waltz with himself. Moving, gliding with a madman's grace. His eyes closed shut while moving to a tune only he can hear. His lips are moving slightly, whispering to himself, perhaps singing a tune to himself. He's back to being the Justin that Davis knew.

The Justin from the bar in LA.

Slick as hell. Dressed in a dark, smart suit and a crisp, white shirt with a bloodred silk tie that sways as his body moves to an unheard rhythm. Not a hair out of place, with the custom-tailored threads clinging to his athletic build. His Italian shoes shine in the moonlight as they glide over the grass, shuffling among the leaves.

Davis pauses for a moment to watch. Rational thoughts escape him as his fear grips him tighter and tighter. He squeezes his fists, not sure if his nails have broken skin. He feels his fear turning fast however.

Turning to anger.

He can't believe how calm this man is, dancing alone in the woods in the dead of night as if the world simply did not exist. In complete control of the chaos he's created. The proverbial eye of the storm. Davis feels anger ball up in his stomach. His mind shifts to a much different place. He's done marveling at the mental state of this man. This cancer.

This Justin.

He looks into the bag he has thrown over his shoulder one last time. Checks the contents. Rubs his hand on the leather, thinking of the papers that rest safely inside. The plan rips through his jumbled thoughts. He's thought it through. Talked it through with Todd. This plan, it has to work. There is no backup. Nothing to try next and no way to turn back if it doesn't. If this does not work, there is nothing.

Davis clears his throat.

Justin puts up a finger, requesting a moment, not bothering to look up, as if he knew the whole time Davis was there. He spins, sways, then slides his feet together for a final pose, holding it for a silent count, then takes a bow. After a long pause, Justin rises up, looking slightly disappointed there was no applause.

Davis moves closer to him, folding the map up and stuffing it into his back pocket.

"They don't have clocks back at the house?" Justin asks.

Davis stares.

"Late. You. You're late. That's what I'm saying about you."

"I had to wait. I couldn't just—"

"Just screwin' with ya. Relax, man." Justin eyes the bag. "Whatcha got there? My goddamn money? Perhaps? Maybe?"

"No."

"No?"

"No."

"Oh no," Justin says with a playful frown. "So I

guess you've decided to do something else for me. Plan B."

Davis's teeth grind.

"Didn't see you going that route." Justin giggles. "I mean I get it, right? You do a dirty deed, then it's over. Boom. Murder is less of a hassle than sneaking money around from the wife and all that skeezy shit."

Each word digs into Davis's thoughts, boring their way inside, taking up residence in his brain. Worming their way in and out, digging deeper and deeper. Justin holds up a hand and nods as if he's figured something out that's been eating at him.

"Wait. I get it."

"What?" Davis says between clinched teeth.

"Well, I guess you do have a taste for it now. Don't you, killer?"

"That's..." Davis's tongue gets tangled in the words. "That's a lie."

"Not sure it's a lie, Big Fun. I mean, I wasn't there, of course. I was in spirit, always in spirit, but I wasn't actually in the room."

"Stop."

"They say the best memories are the ones we forget."

Davis feels off-balance. His mind spins through the images from his phone, all of them, landing on the one of Tilley dead on the floor. This time, Davis's mind adds movement to the image. He can see the blood pouring from her throat. Imagines the sounds she made. Gasping. Fighting for a last bit of air. Last bit of life.

"Look, man. You're the one who wanted to get college-girl drunk that night."

"Stop talking."

"I think you need to talk about it. Talking helps. It's damn healthy, even. Lets you get all that shit out."

Justin inches closer, his words becoming sharper, hitting harder. Davis steps back, only to find his back against something. He's been backed up into a tree. Justin stops only a foot away from him, cocks his head birdlike, studying Davis. He seems to be thinking something over. Analyzing. Creating. Picking away at an idea.

Justin's eyes flare. His lips curl. Davis can almost see Justin's mind lock and load, latching onto an idea. A ringside seat to Justin's brain landing on something that excites him. There's a spark. Davis can see it. Something horrible is pacing back and forth behind Justin's pulsing eyes.

Justin's face lights up.

"Did Tilley scream? Did she fight?" Justin snaps his fingers. "Wait, you did it while she was sleeping, didn't you?" He claps his hands together with glee. "You did. You sick bastard."

"No." Davis turns away from Justin. "That's not what happened," he whispers to himself.

"Just tell me one more thing."

"Stop," Davis says louder.

"I gotta know."

"Just don't, please."

Justin claps his hands, jumping back and bouncing on the balls of his feet, then stops cold, standing straight, like a well-dressed exclamation point. He licks his lips, taking a pause for dramatic effect.

"Tell me." Justin points a finger toward Davis. "When you killed her, did she squeal like she did when you fucked her?"

A fire ignites inside Davis. He launches from the tree, charging hard at Justin with all that he has. Fueled by an untapped rage that's been kept stowed away for way too long.

Justin barely blinks. Barely moves. He makes a quick tilt right then grabs Davis by the shirt, tossing him aside like a bag of trash. Davis fumbles over his feet, skids into the dirt, then rolls to a stop.

"Okay, that was crass. Perhaps too much. I can admit that." Justin flips his hair back. "Apologies. Sometimes I shouldn't say everything in my head." He helps Davis to his feet, brushing off the leaves and dirt. "Daddy called it the gumball disease. You know, like every idea drops from your brain to your tongue like a gumball machine."

Davis pushes him away, clinging to his bag.

"Now. Enough with the kicking each other in

the nuts." Justin eyes the bag. "Let's have a look at whatcha got in that bag of yours."

Davis feels his stomach tighten. His mouth goes dry. He wants to give him the bag, but he knows that once he does it's going to start a war that he might not win. A bonfire that will lead either to his freedom or his destruction.

"Well? Is this your way of building up some drama?" Justin waits with his hand out. "Don't bother. You're better than that."

Davis thinks of his girls. Of Hattie. Of everything he's worked to build in this life.

He throws the bag at Justin. It lands hard to Justin's chest. The force makes him take a step back. Justin raises his eyebrows, faking being impressed with the force of the toss.

Davis's eyes bounce as he watches Justin rifle through the bag. His eyes scan documents, his lips moving while he reads over the dense paragraphs. Davis can see the arrogant bullshit that Justin was lathered in only moments ago fading away into the night. Something in his face has dulled. Maybe only slightly, but that wild energy surging inside him isn't as strong as it was.

Davis permits a smile. This is going to work. He can feel it.

Davis thinks of killing him right now, while he's preoccupied. He shakes his head, surprised by his own thoughts. He's never considered the possibility until now—taking another man's life. In a flash of imagination, he envisions himself bashing Justin's head into a tree over and over again. He can hear the crunch of Justin's skull inside his own thoughts. The spitting of blood. The gargled moans of pain after the dull thumps of bark. The satisfaction. Davis plays it all out in his mind without an ounce of effort.

Is this what I've become?

Am I a violent man? Am I capable of what those pictures showed?

For the first time, he considers the idea that maybe he did it. Maybe he did it all.

Maybe he killed Tilley.

Did I?

No. There's no way he could have done that. The very idea of killing her, in that way, makes him sick even now. He thinks of taking a knife and slicing a person's throat. The act of it. The physical mechanics of it. The sights. The sounds. The feeling of steel on skin. The cutting. As his mind churns, he can't help but feel some familiarity.

Is this imagination or memory?

In a brief moment of passion, did something set him off while he was under the influence of whatever drugs they used on him? Was he crazed with chemicals, booze and lust? Did he simply make the move, void of any thought or conscience? If he can stand here and think of killing Justin, then maybe he could have done the same with Tilley.

"No," he whispers to himself.

An image of Tilley pops into his mind. He squeezes his eyes shut.

Justin flips through the pages.

Tilley on her back, moaning with pleasure. She licks her lips then sucks his finger. The initial rush. The spark in her eyes as he enters her.

Davis squeezes his eyes tighter.

Pages flip one after another.

Tilley's eyes open wide, her mouth fighting for air as the blood floods from her throat.

Davis wraps his face in his hands, runs his fingers through his hair, now slick with sweat.

He sees her throat split. The blood spits and spurts out onto the floor. Tilley's naked body flops and twists as she grabs her neck, deep red spilling between her fingers. She looks up toward Davis. *Help,* she mouths silently.

"What hell is all this shit?" Justin asks.

Davis snaps from his trance. Shaken by his own mind, he pulls himself together, finding his place in the here and now.

"It's all there," he says, clearing his throat.

"Really?" Justin asks, scrunching up his nose. "That's damn disappointing."

Justin slams his fist into Davis's face.

31

Davis stumbles back.

His eyes blur with tears as he feels his sinuses flood. The blood rolls down from his nose, streaming over his lips. He plants his hand on a tree for stability.

Another fist screams toward his head.

Davis pivots enough to avoid a full-on strike. Justin's fist grazes his ear, the main force of the blow only finding the night air. Davis grabs Justin's arm, shoving him back. He swings wildly, landing a punch to the side of Justin's cheek.

Justin swats his second punch away like an airborne nuisance.

Twisting away, Davis straightens his back, only to have a punishing gut punch land hard, removing all the air from his lungs. Davis folds as if he were

Justin's laundry. He fights again to find air, his throat raw from coughing, his lungs burning.

Justin leans down, positioning his mouth directly next to Davis's ear, shushing him, rubbing his back as if comforting a sick child, like he did on the pier earlier.

"If you're broke, how in the sweet name of Christ is my investment in you supposed to pay off?" Justin lifts Davis's chin with his fingers, meeting his eyes. "Do you understand my problem here? I've put some serious time and resources into you." Justin holds his eyes like he's looking through them, staring into the mind behind them. "When I start a thing, I always ask, 'what does the question cost?' You're a question to me and the question was, and still is, 'what's it going to cost me to get the most from his life?'" Justin lowers his chin with a smile. "And, if your life is worth more than the cost of the question, then I move forward with that thing."

Davis pushes Justin off of him, moving a few feet away.

Justin moves up fast, closing the distance between them. He grabs Davis's shoulders and squeezes tight. "You started with a question too, Davis. In LA, you wanted to know if I could deliver the time of your life. And that, buddy, is an expensive question."

Davis plants his palms to Justin's chest, sending him back a couple of steps.

"I didn't ask you for this."

"Maybe you did, maybe you didn't."

"I never wanted one of your damn packages."

"Really? You sure?"

"Stay away from me."

"That's cute," Justin says, moving toward him.

"Not warning you again. We can finish this right here, right now. Maybe you'll even kill me. But let's be clear... maybe, just maybe you won't."

Justin nods, looking up toward the stars.

Davis digs in, widening his stance, preparing.

"Okay." Justin clucks his tongue. "How about we skip all that shit and head straight to threatening your family."

Davis's eyes go wide.

"You're smart and shit. Put that big brain to work and think. What do you think I could do to them? To Hattie, to your pretty little girls?"

The blood in Davis's veins slows to a crawl as his vision narrows to a slit, only seeing Justin framed in a fuzzy background. It's as if the entire world has been blurred out, and now it's only the two of them. Two men squared off under the moonlight, isolated in the woods. A random encounter at a bar in Los Angeles has led them both here. A chance meeting that has turned into a nightmare.

"That's the next play, right?" Justin says. "The escalation of things. You had to see that shit coming, right?"

Justin cocks his head, looking Davis over with his eyebrows raised.

"You didn't, did you?" Justin laughs. "Oh my God, you really didn't think that was a possibility. You are goddam adorable."

Davis lunges at Justin.

An immediate loss of control. Removed. Stripped away from him. Davis lands a shoulder into Justin's gut, sending them both flying hard into a tree. Justin's back crunches upon impact with the bark. Davis feels all the air leave Justin's body. He feels the sudden satisfaction of imposing some will on this man. He lands a punch, then another and another. A surge of adrenaline rips through him.

It's short-lived, however.

Justin tosses him back, working a series of left and right punches like a skilled prizefighter. A brief but steady drumbeat of pops and thumps landing one after the other. Davis blocks one, then misses the second and third. He feels his knees buckle, comes close to stumbling to the ground, but finds the strength to throw a punch with all he has.

His fist finds the side of Justin's face. Davis feels Justin's jaw give. His hand cracks upon impact. The spike of pain is intense, but it doesn't dull what he sees in front of him. Davis watches as Justin falls away off the force of his blow.

Davis hurt him.

Justin spins toward the dirt but places a hand down and pushes himself up. As he comes up, there's a massive smile on his face. A slight trickle of blood makes its way down his chin.

"You've got some fine-ass spirit, Big Fun." Justin pulls a red, silk handkerchief from his suit pocket dabbing it at his lip. "Is this what you want to do? Like you said, we can work this all out right here. Right now."

Davis readies himself. Raises his fists.

"You know the difference between normal people and psychopaths, Davis?" Justin asks. "We simply want things more than you."

Justin raises his hands as well, starting to bounce on the balls of his feet. He looks like he did on the pier with Hattie and the girls. Davis stops.

Think.

Davis knows the truth. He was lucky just now. His best punch was lucky, and it only slowed him down briefly. Davis has no weapons and he's beyond outmatched in a hand-to-hand fight with this man.

He knows what he said about working this out right here and now, but he needs to fight this guy smarter. Not like this. He has to take a beat and push down his basic male instincts. The burning need to release his anger, to calm his fear with his fists. He wants nothing more than to unleash, to beat the life out of Justin with his bare hands, but he knows that's not the smart play.

Think.

There's a lot at stake here. A lot on the table if he starts a war he can't win out here in the woods. The upside in winning is unlikely. The downside is unthinkable. If Justin wins, if he beats Davis into coma or even kills him, he's not going to stop at just Davis. A man like Justin doesn't know how to quit. He'll go after Hattie and the girls even if Davis is out of the picture. Davis knows he will.

Justin will not stop.

Ever.

Think.

Davis knows he needs to buy himself time, and if he goes toe to toe with Justin then time will be up for him and his family. Davis lowers his hands, letting them fall to his sides.

"Nobody wins a war," Davis says. "Talk?"

"Sure."

"You and I, we're businessmen, right?"

"I'm willing to speculate, yes."

"This doesn't have to go this way. We can work out something, but those documents in that bag are telling you the truth."

Justin rolls his eyes.

"It's true, Justin. I don't have any damn money."

"And according to those fancy papers you don't even own any of the company anymore. That correct as well?"

Davis nods. "I had to sell out to make up for paying what I've already paid you. I was broke before I met you."

"So you lied to me in LA." Justin shakes his head. "All that shit about how well you're doing." He waves his hands wildly, mocking the thought. *"Ooooh look at me. I'm a big-time tech guy. My company is so mind-bending* and blah, blah-blah, blah-blah."

Davis nods again, giving him nothing, not taking the bait.

Justin settles in, standing still, letting the silence fill in the gaps.

"Well," he finally says, "what in the hell are we going to do about this little pickle?"

Justin begins to pace. Davis's heart thumps, waiting for Justin's next move, but he doesn't want to say anything. Doesn't want to give Justin anything to work with. He's already given him too much, he knows.

"Okay. Final offer. You pay me one hundred thousand or, of course, you can kill someone of my choosing."

"What?" Davis's mouth goes instantly dry.

"Is it the killing someone? You seem really reluctant to that option."

Davis stares in disbelief. They're going backward.

"It's the easiest out for you," Justin says, "but you keep tripping over it."

"You've seen the documents. I don't have a hundred grand."

"I'm not negotiating on this. This is a firm offer."

"That's insane. How can I—"

Justin puts a hand up. "Don't feel like you need to answer me right away. No pressure. Sleep on it. Give it a think. Meet me here, same time tomorrow night."

Davis stands lifeless, can only stare back. A silent statue under the stars.

"Glad we did this."

And with that, Justin slips off into the night.

32

Davis slips back in through the front door.

The house is dark. The quiet feels eerie. A wall of silence so void of sound it buzzes.

He brushed himself off the best he could outside, even removed his shirt and shoes before he crept back inside the house. As he carefully makes his way toward the back of the house, he hears the soft, wonderful sound of his girls snoring in their room. The noise fills him with joy and dread all at the same time.

The idea that Justin is out there. Wandering somewhere in the night. The thought that he can come in here, inside this house, whenever he wants is chilling. The idea tugs at Davis's guts. He checks the locks again, knowing that it doesn't really matter.

Moving as slowly and as quietly as he can,

Davis slips into the bathroom. Shutting the door behind him, he turns on the light. His face is red and well on its way to swollen, with specs of dirt and debris peppering spots on his forehead and cheeks. The blood from his nose is starting to dry into clumps of black candy under his nostrils. His hands ache from the punches that connected, while his head and body throb from the punches he's absorbed.

Turning on the water, he cups his hands under the faucet. The first splash stings like a son of a bitch to his cut and battered bare hands. He pulls them back, then places them back under the streaming water. With each passing second, the sting gets a little better, the pain becoming easier to live with. He breathes out, waiting for the collection of pains to subside. The seconds crawl. He counts softly to himself, letting the falling numbers help the moments pass. Letting time tumble away. The seconds slip by, then another and the next.

As he tries to pull himself together, his mind churns. A cranking brain has been the norm lately, his new normal, but this time he's thankful for the buckshot nature of his thinking. It's allowing him to focus on something other than the physical damage, even if that means focusing on the mental.

It's what passes for peace right now.

Davis has to get ahold of Todd. He'll try him as soon as he gets out of the bathroom, but he has to give Todd this new info. Justin's *final offer*. He needs to talk through what they can do next. It's hard to call his meeting with Justin a success, but it wasn't a complete failure either. Davis didn't crumble, even when Justin pushed buttons beyond reason. He took a beating but laid down some of his own. More importantly, Davis got his point across. The main point. He got Justin to understand that he's broke and the business is out of play.

Still, Justin's counteroffer is insane. If that's even a counteroffer at all.

Justin likes his games.

Davis tries to ignore the "kill someone" offer—Justin does say crazy things—but the hundred-thousand-dollar payment to make Justin go away is the one that sticks in Davis's brain. That seems like a well thought out number. It was something in the way he said it, in the way he talked about the cost of a question and all that. This is a business to Justin, nothing more. That number is something Justin has calculated. Something real. A number that was derived from his sick profit and loss statement.

Could that number buy my freedom?

Todd could get the hundred grand. It would hurt probably, or maybe it wouldn't, but Todd could find it if he had to.

Davis can't believe he's even considering this as an option.

In his heart, he knows that even if they pay the hundred grand to a man like Justin, he will not simply go away. Even if Davis agreed to kill someone, Justin would not simply go away. He can see it in Justin's eyes; he's not going anywhere. That man will bleed Davis dry until there is nothing left and then move on to the next victim. In Justin's mind, he's thinking that if Davis can come up with a hundred then he can come up with two, then three, and so on and so on. This is what Justin does. He told him so.

Justin the predator. The parasite.

A psychopath who simply wants things more than Davis does.

33

———

The sun peeks through a break between the curtains.

Davis stares bleary-eyed at the wall, watching shadows retreat. He hasn't slept. He's simply been lying there, staring with eyes wide.

After he felt Hattie get up and leave the bedroom he moved to pacing around the room, moving in quick bursts while his guts churned and his mind raced around an infinite track at blinding speed. He's now back sitting on the edge of the bed looking out into nothing. His thoughts have slammed back and forth against the walls of his skull, bouncing from hope to disaster, from salvation to destruction.

He's been calling, sending texts to Todd all night. Lost count of the number. Nothing from Todd. His phone a lifeless brick of silence.

Davis snickers, thinking how his messages have become akin to him screaming into a flight recorder as his plane is going down. Unloading streams of nouns, verbs and adjectives into the void, only hoping that someone out there will listen. Hoping that someone will offer some help. He gave up about an hour ago, lost track of time, but he knows the entire house will be up soon. He can hear Hattie moving around the kitchen, but hasn't heard the girls yet. The sun has just started to rise and the day will begin soon enough.

He doesn't know how he's going to explain his appearance to his family.

He took a couple of shots to the face last night, and he's sure the stress and lack of sleep aren't helping his boyish charm any. Hattie is going to see it. Not just the marks and bruises. She'll see under his skin. She's going to know that all of this, his mood, his odd behavior, is far more than just problems with the business. Business stress does not lend itself to a swollen face beaten by punches or the distance in his eyes that he can no longer hide.

She's going to know. She can probably sense it right now. Probably has for days. Hattie knows Davis better than Davis knows himself. Add that to her devastating, no-bullshit intelligence and she will force him into the truth or walk out on him. Either one will level Davis to the floor.

How do I tell her?

Where the hell do I even begin?

The crazy thing is, Davis still isn't even completely sure he did anything wrong. He's seen the pictures, but there's a disconnect from what he's seeing and what he knows about himself. He can't trust his mind, his memories or his mental state, which is deteriorating by the second. He sure as hell can't trust anything Justin is giving him either. The truth is uncertain.

Tilley's image rips through his head.

He grinds his teeth.

She moans.

He buries his head in his pillow, rocking back and forth.

She screams.

He sees himself in the hotel room standing above her with a knife in his shaking hand, blood shining from the edge of the blade. Even here in this lake house's bedroom, he knows the feelings of that night.

Are these feelings real?

Davis lies down, covers his face with a pillow. Tries to block the bad things from storming his head. More tricks from a battered brain.

That night, with the knife held tight in his hand, is that sensation similar to the rush he felt when he first met Tilley in the hotel bar? Is he merely projecting in order to try and understand?

No, that's not the truth. Davis knows it. This is

no projection or an attempt to understand. To be more accurate, to be more honest, this feeling is a memory. This is too real, too precise. The feeling he is getting from thinking of the knife in his hand is coming in loud and clear. This is the same feeling he felt when he was on top of her. When he slid inside of her.

An undeniable charge of life.

Excitement mixed with something else. Something with teeth. Biting. Present. A heightened feeling of regret mixed with a bolt of electricity. As if he'd done something. Accomplished something. Ended something. It was a feeling of power, then devastating sadness. He remembers a hand on his shoulder.

He remembers dropping the knife.

Davis's phone buzzes next to him on the bed.

TODD lights up on the screen.

34

Davis's fingers fumble, scrambling into the wadded-up sheets, snatching up the phone.

"Where the hell have you been?" Davis barks, fighting to keep his voice down.

There's a pause on Todd's side, followed by a deep sigh. A long beat of silence.

"Okay," Todd finally says, "you're going to go through two things pretty quickly—"

"Cut the shit, Todd. Tell me something good. You'd better have something really, really good."

"Please. Hear me out."

Davis resets, grinds his teeth together and exhales hard through his nose. There's something in the way Todd is speaking. His voice is not the same as usual. His tone is different. His word choice off. None of it normal.

"Two things," Todd says. "One. You are going

to be very, very upset with me. Two. You're also going to be very, very rich."

Davis feels his heart skip a row of beats. He can't begin to form the words needed to ask a rational question. His mouth and tongue are failing him, fumbling over any form of communication with his friend.

"You still there?" Todd asks.

"Yeah," Davis barely gets out. "I'm here."

There's another audible sigh from Todd followed by a deep breath. "That investment firm I've been talking to you about? I sold the company." Todd stops speaking, lets his words hang in the air.

Davis can't even process what's just been said.

"I tried to talk to you about this, but..." Todd stops, then starts again. "They're a huge money manager with a massive quant model they use for picking stocks. They're going to use the language software, the one you built, and fold it into their model. Use it as part of a way to predict earnings based on CEO speech patterns or some shit. All with your language algorithm. They paid us more than the original offer. A lot more."

Davis feels himself drop as if thrown from a building. Then comes the sensation of floating above the bed. It's as if he's not here, no longer a part of this world. The thoughts running around his head are now spinning out of control, whipping into a dizzying blur of random, useless characters and pictures of pictures. It's as if he's floating, watching himself from above, watching someone else have this conversation with Todd. Davis imagines that he isn't even in the room. He's drifting like a kite above the house looking down, but listening to everything.

"Davis, I know you're beyond pissed at me right now, I get it, but hear this." Todd pauses for effect. "You will never have a single money problem ever again. Let that sink in, man."

Upset, Davis thinks. *He said I'd be upset.*

"The money from the sale is tied up right now with all the contract and lawyer shit. It'll be a few days before we get it, but the deal, it's all done. They're going to pay us each a fat eight-figure check, and then keep us on as advisors." He sucks in a breath. "Davis, salary of a hundred and fifty grand. That's in addition to the multi-million-dollar cash dump. Are you listening to me, man?" Todd waits. "You're going to be stupid rich."

Todd's words barely land, bouncing off like rain.

"You can take that money and go create something else even better than what we just sold. You're free. You can do whatever you want in this life."

Davis can't even process what his friend has done to the business.

To him.

"Hattie can quit, or do whatever she wants. The girls' college is taken care of. You? You are free from all that mental money shit you've been hauling around."

Davis starts working through the timeline in his head.

"You hear me, Davis? The future is limitless."

Todd got full control of the company and took advantage of the situation. Did what he's been wanting to do all along.

"Will you say something?" Todd asks.

Todd used him. Somehow he pulled the strings to all of this. The dots aren't all connecting yet, but Davis knows he's been betrayed by his trusted friend. Manipulated somehow into a business deal he never agreed to. Davis feels the bubbling rage rising up inside of him.

"Please?" Todd begs.

Then it hits him.

Todd pulled off what he's said he loves doing, pulled off the best kind of sale. He got the other guy to think it was their idea. He got Davis to think of signing it all over to Todd. That allowed Todd to do what he did. Davis telling Todd to draw up the paperwork and fast-track the legal docs unknowingly helped set all this up for Todd. He handed Todd the keys to the kingdom and Todd wasted no time getting what he wanted.

How long has he been planning this, piecing this together?

Had Todd been working this angle before LA, or did he wait until Justin helped provide an opening? A crack. An angle to exploit. Is there a difference between Justin and Todd? Two people who simply want it more.

Davis feels the inside of his mouth turn to dust, dry as a desert. Disbelief firing through every part of him.

How could I be so stupid?

"What have you done?" Davis finally asks.

"Davis—"

"What did you do?"

"I did what I thought was best for both of us."

"By blowing up everything we're doing?"

"Davis, think about—"

"You've sold us out. We're a commodity now. You made us a piece of someone else's robot."

"You're upset—"

"There's that word again. Upset. Of course I'm fucking upset you fucking asshole. You sold us to a company, a corporation. The very thing we were trying to leave in the first place. Don't you get that? You destroyed what we made."

"I made us rich."

That stops Davis cold.

"You were sending us to bankruptcy, and I made us rich."

The words hit him hard. The truth of his friend's words hurt more than Davis could ever imagine. Todd betrayed him, there's no way around that, but Davis can't question the result. The business was failing, and Davis wasn't doing much to help it. He may never forgive Todd, their friendship is probably beyond repair, and he certainly will never trust him again. But as Davis's shock and anger fades a bit, there's a sense of calm coming over him as he starts to process.

He doesn't have to worry about the business anymore. The idea that money is no longer a problem is difficult for him to get his head around, hard to imagine. He's devoted most of his adult life to worrying about money. Stretching it. Not having enough of it. Not providing the right life for his family. Failing them and himself.

With all this new information plowing through his broken mind at such a high velocity, he'd almost forgotten the situation he's in. Almost forgotten about Justin. His beaten mind failed to realize the obvious – with the money from this deal he can shake this guy off of him.

"When will the deal close?" Davis asks.

"Look, there's more, a lot more. I've been driving all night to get there. That's why you couldn't get ahold of me."

"There? Where are you?"

Another pause on Todd's end of the conversation.

"There are some parts to this that need to be said in person, for several reasons."

"You're here in town?"

"Come out and meet me. We need to talk face-to-face. Found a coffee joint. Not like our normal spot, but it'll do. Meet me. Now would be good," Todd says. "Please."

The word *please* stabs into Davis. Not a word Todd uses.

Davis throws on some clothes, not completely sure what he has on.

Doesn't care.

Grabbing his keys, as quietly as he can he slips out from the room. The girls' door is still closed and there's no sign of activity in the house. It's still fairly early, so maybe Hattie decided to lie back down with them. Or maybe she's in there helping them get dressed. Either way, Davis sees an opportunity to slip out without them seeing him in the state he's in. He knows his face is a battered mess. Last thing he wants to do right now is explain his appearance. Create another line of lies.

Davis moves in long, silent strides across the living room floor, wanting to maximize his efficiency to the door. His muscles burn and ache. He can still feel his face swell and pulse. The knuckles on his hands are misshaped masses of various colors. He can barely feel his right hand as it holds his keys.

He closes the front door carefully, making as little noise as possible. He stops for a second, then looks down toward the pier. He wants to be sure that his family isn't out there again. To see they are not down there, and to make sure Justin is not there either.

No sign of Hattie or the girls.

He locks the door.

He pulls his phone out as he slides into the driver's seat and sends a text to Hattie, thinking he still needs to cover himself in case they come out of the room too soon.

I wanted to get out of the house and get some air. I'll be back soon.

He's not sure what this face-to-face talk with Todd is going to yield, but there's a feeling of uneasy calm coming over him. He imagines this is how terminal patients must feel toward the end of road. Sad to be at the end, but glad the pain will stop. After all the misery, he can rest soon. When the fight is over he can maybe find some form of peace. This is all coming to an end.

One way or another.

35

THE DINER RESTS out on the edge of Lake Oswego.

The place is packed, buzzing with a morning rush of sorts. Davis was forced to find a spot behind the coffee house near where the employees park by the dumpster.

Davis steps in and the bell above the door chimes. It's a cozy place, nestled in the woods with a great view of the water. The inside is small and tight, but still feels inviting and homey. Dark, rich, wood walls and tables are filled with locals and tourists alike enjoying the simplicity of a family-owned diner. Smells of roasted coffee drift and mix with the tantalizing scent of freshly cooked bacon.

He breathes in the smells of the place. It's the first time in days he remembers smelling anything. He must be feeling better. Or he's finally losing his grip on reality. Giving up. Letting go of it all. Davis doesn't know which, but seeing Todd at the back of the place staring out at the gorgeous picture window view of the rippling lake doesn't help keep his warm and fuzzies around very long.

Davis stands at the door watching his former business partner, his former trusted friend, who sits there shoving eggs and bacon into his face as if this was any other day. As if nothing was wrong and this was just another meeting between them.

It is not.

Today is the day Davis learned his friend betrayed him. Davis isn't even thinking about the money now. Deep down he knows time will heal this wound, and that mountain of money will certainly help speed up that process. But right now? Right now Davis is more than a little pissed off.

There's more to this story. Davis knows it. Something deep and dark.

He tried not to think of what Todd wanted to tell him, what he needed to say in person. Davis wanted to walk in here cold, with as clear a mind as possible and have Todd explain it to him. Whatever it is, Todd drove here through the night and wanted to say it to Davis's face. Davis couldn't help it however. He thought about Todd's visit here over and over again on the drive here. There are really only a few things it could be, none of them good.

Davis balls up his fists.

Todd snaps off a bite of bacon.

Davis burns.

Todd turns, finally noticing his *friend* standing in the doorway. His face drops, then perks up into something forced. Pasted-on happy. He motions for Davis to come over and sit down with him. Taking in a deep breath, Davis moves to the table, taking a seat across from Todd. Davis's back is straight, as if propped up by a slab of steel. His shoulders are gaining tension by the second.

They sit without speaking. The sounds of the coffee joint buzz and chime around them. Davis recalls this same feeling in the air with his family.

A kindly older woman asks Davis if he'd like some coffee as she pours, filling his cup, then leaves without requiring an answer from him. He pours in some cream and stirs, working his coffee to the perfect caramel color. This is their ritual, their coffeehouse meeting routine. Davis remembers the first time they sat down like this back home.

They ended up at that coffee place because it was convenient, really. There was no big discussion as to where they should meet on a regular basis; it was simply where they happened to end up. That first meeting was about leaving their jobs, about walking away from the corporate hell. They laughed and carried on like children, running through ridiculous scenarios. Fantasies of tearing down cube walls, dancing on desks and causing a major scene, along with other forms of workplace mayhem.

It was fun. It was exciting.

This meeting, the one they're having now, is anything but that. Neither of them could possibly have envisioned they would end up like this. Davis stirs his coffee, his insides becoming volcano-like. He can't believe it's come to this.

Todd leans in. "You gonna to talk to me?"

Davis watches the coffee swirl inside the thick, off-white mug, spinning into an almost pleasing color. Close to caramel-colored perfection, but not there yet.

"I know you're mad as hell, I get it, but this can still be a good thing."

Davis adds a touch more cream, then stirs some more.

"Come on, man. Say something, for Christ's sake."

Coffee looks perfect.

Davis looks up.

"When did you put Justin on me?" Davis sips his perfectly colored coffee.

Todd's face goes blank. All bravado lost, torn away from him. Arrogance wiped clean. A man stripped of his armor, left with only an expression-less slate. There's no denial, no defenses to throw at this or excuses to be made. He closes his eyes and leans back in his chair, letting the jab of the question sting.

The kindly older woman returns, refilling their coffee. She offers Davis a menu.

"Only coffee for me, thanks. I'm not eating." He turns, motions his hand across the table. "Todd? Hungry?"

Todd shakes his head, pushing his plate aside. As she leaves, Davis adds more cream to return the balance. This is the first time he's felt in true control of a conversation with Todd. With anyone, really. He hates that he likes it so much.

"Tell me you didn't know what he was." With each word Davis speaks, his rage bubbles and pops, barely containing it underneath his skin. "I want you to explain when you thought inserting that man into my life was good idea."

"I didn't realize what he was going to do, how far he was going to go. That woman..." He stops, then starts again. "The offer from the investment company was in serious jeopardy. Time was—"

"You took the leash off that animal. Bad things have happened. Because of you. You've put my family in danger, you piece of shit. My family!"

Davis slams his palm down to the table. His coffee jumps. So does Todd. Davis fights to get ahold of himself. He needs to understand, and him losing it here won't help anything. He breathes in and out, glancing toward the lake. "What did you think was going to happen? What the hell, man?"

"There's another software package out in the market, an app, cloud-based, not too unlike ours. Similar guts as yours. Not as good, but not far off. The investment company was looking at them as a backup if things didn't work out with us." Todd pauses. "It was a lot of money, Davis. It *is* a lot of money. The kind of money that could get everybody to good."

Getting to good is a concept they've always talked about, even from the beginning. Making enough money so that everybody is all set. *All good.* He's gone back to this idea a lot lately as he's thought about Hattie, the girls, and his family's financial situation.

Can we ever get to good? Is it even possible?

"I got desperate and made a move. It was wrong. I should have looked into that guy more. Hell, I should have talked to you more about it instead of getting that guy in the first place," Todd says, looking down. "I know it doesn't mean shit, but I am sorry."

Davis wipes up the spilled coffee from the table and sips from his cup, letting Todd talk. He wants to hear it spill out from him, knows that Todd is dying to be free of it all. He can tell. Todd's probably kept it all bottled up for a long while. Davis has become way too familiar recently with holding the truth back. Familiar with the weight of it all.

"I talked to a buddy from college. Hedge fund guy. He's used Justin in the past for... *things*. He said the guy was discreet and professional and he would adapt to whatever I wanted."

Davis feels the anger surge up again, but pushes it back down.

"Before your trip to LA, I called him and told him to show you a good time. A real good time." Todd stops, tilts his head away toward the window, unable to look Davis in the eyes. "Maybe get some pictures, charge you some money to make them go away." Todd swallows hard, as if saying the words out loud made it all too real.

Davis wants him to say more. "And?"

"And what?" Todd asks. "Isn't that enough?"

"No. You need to tell me why you chose that."

"What?"

"You need to explain to me why you went with that. That plan. Why the money? You could've gone a thousand directions."

Todd can't turn his way. He picks at his napkin, then his spoon.

"Tell me. You wanted to talk face-to-face, right? I'm here. Talk to me about how you knew that would work. How you told him that I didn't have the money. That I'd crumble. That I'd fall apart because I don't have that kind of money."

Todd squirms.

"That was it, right? That was the key to the plan. Using the financial problems of my past against me. Weaponize my love for my family. Am I missing something?"

"No," Todd says, almost inaudible.

"What was that?"

"No, that's pretty much it."

Davis pushes away from the table and stands, looks down at Todd. A fire blazing inside of him. His fists are balled up against his sides, struggling to hold them back.

"This is over. Call your dog off of me. Do whatever you have to do, but I don't want to be anywhere near you." Davis makes it about two steps then stops, turning back. "And, oh yeah, make sure I get my share of that damn money."

Davis leaves, heading toward the door.

"Wait," Todd calls out.

Davis shoves open the door, cutting through the people outside, charging toward his car. His blood boils. His body shakes as the anger-fueled adrenaline rips through every part of him.

"Davis," Todd calls out again, following behind him. "Come on, man."

Davis reaches his car parked behind the diner. He knows that he's going to have to have at least one more conversation with Todd. He's only a few steps from reaching him. It's going to be unavoidable. For a flash of a thought, Davis considers bashing his head in with the car door.

But he doesn't.

Davis turns around and finds Todd standing in front of him, slightly out of breath.

"You have every reason to hate me," Todd says, "but let me make this right."

Davis listens, but gives him nothing in return.

"I can stop Justin," Todd says. "It's one of the reasons I'm here."

"You've talked to him?"

Todd nods.

"And?"

"I think we've come to an agreement. He's a serious asshole, but I think I talked him into an arrangement that'll end all of this without anything —the pictures, any of it—getting out."

Davis feels an enormous weight lift from his body and mind, as if he's been walking around hauling massive bags of sand ever since LA. He thinks of Tilley.

Am I really going to let money cover that up? Is that what I've become?

His eyes well. He gasps, coughs, then laughs. He can't control it. The release of it all triggered a response in him, one he didn't expect. He leans over, placing his hands on his knees and laughs until tears stream down his face. Todd looks around, not sure what he's supposed to do here.

Davis knows he looks insane right now, but doesn't care. The line between laughing and crying is fine. The one between crazy and sane is even thinner. Davis feels like he's teetering between both.

This is over. Justin is gone.

"Getting to good?" Davis says, still looking down as his laughter slows.

"Yeah. Something like that," Todd says.

Davis can hear it. The way Todd forced the words through a crack in his voice. Todd's emotions are taking hold of him. Davis looks up to Todd. His business partner. His friend.

He's a red-faced mess. Unable to speak. Eyes full. Davis is still angry with him, but in this single moment he knows that Todd is truly sorry. It's not just words right now. It's as if what Todd did has finally hit him. He finally understands. They may never be the same, but Davis at least knows that Todd is capable of feeling regret about it all. And that's a start at least. The theory that *time heals all wounds* will without a doubt be put to the test.

"Okay," Davis says, rising up.

Todd nods, fighting back his own tears, rubbing his eyes clean. Todd reaches out to shake hands with Davis.

A blur slams into the side of Todd's head. His body drops to the ground.

It happened so fast Davis couldn't see where it

even came from. So quick his hand is still out waiting to shake Todd's.

Another blur.

Davis's body goes limp.

His world goes dark.

36

———

Davis forces his eyelids to open.

His head is on fire, pounding like a bass drum without any specific rhythm to follow. His vision is a soup-like fog, showing only blobs of smeared colors cut up by thin slivers of light. As he sits up his stomach turns. Quickly, he realizes he did this way too fast and lies back down almost immediately. There's a rush of nausea coupled with a whirling whip-spin inside his head.

He recognizes this feeling. It's familiar. Very similar to when he woke up in LA, but yet different. He can't put his finger on the difference, but this feels more scattered. Muted consciousness. Not nearly as sharp as before at the hotel.

As his eyes drift into focus he can tell he's back at the lake house. The feeling. The smells. He's in the bedroom he's shared, occasionally, with Hattie.

It's dark. It's night now. He can make out the moon through the window, its glow providing the only light to the room. The door is shut.

Did I lose another day?

I was with Todd in the morning, wasn't I?

Having coffee.

Fighting.

Touching his head, he grits his teeth, jerking his hand back. There's a pulsing, swelling lump on the side of his head that's tender to the touch. He rubs his fingers together without looking at them. They're wet. Slippery-thick with what he's guessing is his own blood.

He remembers the blur in the parking lot. Todd's body dropping.

Davis sits up again, ignoring the twist in his guts, the roar in his skull. As he braces himself with his hands on either side of him, his right hand slides a bit in the sheets. They are slick with something. He raises his hand, inspecting his palm through his blurred vision. His hand is covered, shining black in the moonlight. Fingers and palm coated.

Davis sucks in a hard breath, looks down at the bed next to him. There's a dark stain, a large one, pooling up on top of the sheets before soaking in. He pulls back, his eyes ratcheting into hard focus.

Todd's face is frozen, staring up at the ceiling, his head peacefully resting on the pillow next to Davis.

The rest of his body lies a few inches below the pillow. His neck is still pumping a slight gurgle of life, the dark stain in the sheets growing with each passing second.

A pulse of frantic energy surges and Davis pushes himself away, slipping and scrambling, unable to form a sound. He thinks of Tilley. Her throat cut.

Did I do this too?

Davis falls from the bed with a thick thud. He jump-crawls up against the wall. His chest heaves in and out. Deep, hard, short breaths. Body shaking as if it's below zero.

Framed under the moon, Todd's severed head is perfectly placed on the pillow, his body positioned below with his arms crossed over his chest, fingers locked. Peaceful after the violence is over.

Davis hears the sound of footsteps moving toward the bedroom.

A tongue clucks.

"He's up," Justin says to someone in another room. "Showtime."

The door opens and Justin enters the room, stopping just inside the doorway. The lights in the living room are on and Justin's face and body are shrouded in shadow. Davis can tell he's in a suit, hanging on to cool even now as he leans up against the doorjamb with his arms crossed.

Davis can't speak, still unable to release a single

sound from his lips. He wants to scream, wants to tear Justin apart with his bare hands.

He hears his girls scream. His children are afraid. He can hear their terrified voices trailing off like they're being moved outside through the front door.

Davis jumps to his feet, charging hard at Justin. He's off-balance, stumbling, still disoriented from the blow to the head. Justin grabs him by the shoulders, effortlessly flinging him into the living room. Davis skids across the hardwood floor, stopping as he slams into the table. He's blinded by the sudden burst of light flooding into his vision. Davis can now hear the dog barking, closed off in the other bedroom, going insane, scratching at the door.

Justin glides in, then stops by the table. "For the record, we didn't hurt the damn dog. We're not monsters."

He picks up a stack of papers held together with a large black clip. There are colorful strips marking various pages in the document. Pages Justin wanted to have easy access to after reviewing them closely.

"This thing you gave me," Justin says, holding the document over his head like Moses with the Ten Commandments. "I went over it and over it trying to find an angle. Picking at it like a scab. It was annoying, but I couldn't stop, ya know? I was driven like hell to find something for me to use, and I gotta tell ya, I was damn flustered."

He kicks Davis hard in the ribs. All the air leaves him in a single deep cough as the bone-crunch rattles inside of him.

"Then I talked to your boy, Todd. He had a solution to get me to go away. Seemed rather sudden. Damn sudden. And after a few searches I happened upon a blog post on a rather obscure tech site. That obscure tech blog talked about your firm selling out to a rather large investment firm."

"Where's my family?"

"Not yet." Justin fakes a kick then stops as Davis balls up into a childlike defensive position. "The dollar amount this obscure site gave, well, I have to admit it gave me a little surge in my shorts."

"Please."

"Nope. Still talking." Justin starts pacing while giving his sermon. "Then I went back over the papers you provided and it hit me like a hammer from the gods. There's a section called *Transfer Upon Death*. That part didn't get altered. Still says it all goes to you if Todd goes bye-bye." Justin holds his arms out wide. "A real light bulb moment, if ever there was one."

Davis knows what he's going to say before he says it.

"The math on this is simple. If Todd owns everything and I've got nothing on him, then I've got nothing. But I've got everything on you, so if he dies and you get the company..." Justin runs his finger across his throat bladelike. "What's a boy to do?"

Davis pushes himself up onto his knees. He listens toward the front door but doesn't hear his girls anymore. No sign of Hattie anywhere.

"Where are they? What did you do?"

The green-eyed beauty steps in through the front door. She gives Davis a finger-curl hello then scrunches her nose with an affirming nod to Justin. She slinks over next to him, wrapping an arm around his waist.

Davis pushes up hard, getting to his feet and moving toward them. "If you hurt them..."

Justin pulls a gun out from inside his suit jacket then casually hands it the green-eyed beauty. She puts the barrel in her mouth and holds it in like a lollipop, letting her cheeks suck in, then slips it from her lips with a smack.

Davis comes to a dead stop as she places the moist gun barrel between his eyes.

"Let's go outside," Justin says. "Damn stuffy in here."

They push Davis out the door into the driveway. A black BMW not far from the door has its trunk open. The tiny light in the hatch illuminates the inside of the trunk. Inside are Davis's two little girls. Their hands are bound with zip ties, their mouths shut with duct tape, their eyes wide as pies. They are terrified beyond reason, tears tumbling down their trembling faces.

Davis runs toward them.

Justin sticks a foot out, tripping him, letting him stumble and fall into the gravel rocks of the driveway. The green-eyed beauty skips over to the BMW, slams the trunk closed, then tosses the gun over to Justin. She takes a position standing on the larger rocks that line the gravel driveway.

Davis can only stare at the closed trunk, imagining how afraid his girls are inside. Inside in the dark, bound and tied. Strangers with guns on their father. Their helpless father. Pathetically falling to the ground as he tried to save them.

"It's okay," he calls out to them, hoping they can hear him inside. "It's going to be okay."

"It can be," Justin says. "It really can. All it takes is a little bit of money."

The green-eyed beauty snickers.

"Sorry," he says to her, then turns back to Davis. "A lot of money, actually."

"Where's Hattie?" Davis asks, struggling to get himself up to his feet.

Justin checks his phone, then says, "Ooooh, not far."

"What do you want?" Davis asks. "What's the amount?"

"Haven't worked that out yet. Need to know

the final number you'll make off the sale of your business. You people have been less than forthright with numbers so far, so you can understand my reluctance to trust."

"What did you do with my wife?"

"Nothing really. She just went on a ride with a friend. See, we didn't know how long you were going to be out and we needed some privacy to take care of, ya know, Todd."

"I'll pay, I don't care."

Davis says it, but he knows no amount will end this. Nothing has changed. This is the same Justin as always. There isn't a number that will pacify this beast. Davis has to do something. Something unthinkable.

"I know you will, but I wanted you to think hard about what we did to your friend in there. That was what we call in the biz *sending a strong message*. Then I want you to think about what we could do to Hattie if we put our backs into it." He pauses, then points the gun at the trunk and whispers, "Or to them."

"Don't. Point that at me, not them."

"Touching." Justin turns his head slightly as he sees headlights approaching behind them. He tosses the gun between his hands for a moment, finally stopping and holding it steady at Davis. "You've been an interesting one, I gotta say. Challenging and boring all at the same time."

Davis looks to the headlights approaching. Hattie must be in that car. The feeling of helpless rage erupting inside of him is almost too much to take. He wants to charge Justin, get the gun, and put two in each of their heads.

Patience. Think. Wait until Hattie gets here.

"Funny thing, Big Fun," Justin says as another BMW pulls up into the drive, tires rumbling in the rocks. Its windows are blacked out, blocking any view of who's inside. "If you think real, real hard you'll remember something. I told you what I was going to do to you the first time we met."

"What?" Davis asks.

"Give it a good think," Justin says, turning to the car.

The passenger door opens and Hattie steps out. She seems unharmed, but she's afraid. Shaken. Her face is red, possibly from crying, possibly just from the rage. She looks to Davis; her eyes are empty.

Davis breathes a small sigh of relief that she's alive. "Are you okay?"

"No," she says. "But I'm not hurt, if that's what you're asking me."

Justin grabs her arm, pulling her over in front of him. He places the gun to her temple. Davis's heart skips a row of beats.

"You ready for this?" Justin asks.

"No," Davis spits out. "Don't. Wait." He runs, racing toward Justin and Hattie.

The driver's door of the BMW opens.

Davis stops in his tracks. His feet plant, sucked into the gravel.

"So brave," Tilley says as she steps from the car. "Like that. Like that a lot."

Davis stands like a statue.

Shock has seized every muscle.

"You're..." He fumbles around his words. "What? How?"

Tilley glides around the front bumper, moving toward Davis.

Gone is the ultra-sexy sheen she possessed in LA. She still carries her beauty, but no longer wields it like a surgeon's scalpel. She's more muted, more distant now, dressed in a smart business suit with a look that's more ruthless attorney than a woman interested in seduction. She's almost a different person than the one he met at the hotel bar. It's her, but there's a hardness, an unmistakable coldness to her. All the energy and charm she held before has vanished.

She now stands inches in front of Davis,

studying him. He can't help but stare blankly at her throat. Not a scratch. A silver necklace of a butterfly hangs where Davis imagines the cut would have been.

"You're alive," he mutters, more to himself than anything.

Tilley leans in to whisper, making sure the warmth of her breath tickles his ear. "Of course I'm alive, silly. You wouldn't kill anybody." She pulls back, holds his face in her hands and quietly says, "I mean, hell, we couldn't even get you to fuck me." Tilley holds his eyes, then breaks into a smile with a curl of her lip. Slinking away, she takes a seat on the hood of the BMW.

Davis's head swirls into a mental tornado. The images of the pictures he's seen shatter in his mind. Fragments of memories explode then slam back together. Memories he can't begin to trust. Feelings he thought he'd had didn't happen at all, were not real. Not his to begin with. Manufactured by his mind off stories he was told by the insane. His fragile reality is burning down, his own mind betraying him.

Looking to Hattie, his heart snaps in two.

Her face is a twisted mix of confusion and disbelief. Her eyes dance, but her body is as still as a stone. A wax statue of his wife standing, staring past Davis with Justin's gun at her head. Davis doubts she knows the gun is even there. She's staring at the back of the car where her girls are being held.

The trunk thumps. Muted screams sound from inside.

Hattie jumps.

"Easy, Hattie," Justin says into her ear, pulling her back and pressing the gun harder to her temple. "We're almost there. A little trust, please."

Davis steps toward the BMW that holds his daughters.

The green-eyed beauty slides over, taking a seat on the middle of the trunk. She pulls a knife from her pocket, flips open the large blade, then starts picking her nails with the sharp, pointed end.

"What are you doing?" Davis asks, turning between them all. His voice vibrates. "Why? Why do this? They didn't do anything to you. This is all on me. Let them go."

"It's an escalation thing. We need to break you, Big Fun. There are levels to breaking someone down. Lots of variables. The situation. The mental makeup of the person, and so on. In the beginning, in LA, we needed things to use against you in order to perform the task we agreed to take on. To do what we were paid to do by your buddy Todd."

Hattie looks toward Davis. There's something in her eyes. Davis can see it.

"We staged all the sexy, sexy stuff and planned to use that during round one. If we needed to"—

Justin jerks his head toward Tilley—"we'd move on to the pics of you killing her. Turns out we needed to. As you know."

Davis checks Hattie. Her expression hasn't changed. She's not even listening to them. She's dialed into something inside her own head.

"Those were fun to do," Tilley says to her.

"They were, weren't they?" Justin says, coming back to Davis. "You see, right? An escalation of blackmail to achieve a goal."

Davis looks to Hattie. He knows her. Her brain is churning, working a plan.

"We're way past pictures now. This is different, a special set of circumstances," Justin says. "The money we're talking about now is far too big for that shit. Now we're talking *daughters in a trunk and a gun to a wife's head* type money. Congrats, man. You're moving on up."

Hattie locks eyes with Davis.

She bites her lower lip.

She's using our signal.

Their wordless signal that something needs to be done. Davis fights to not show anything on his face.

"Listen now. We're running a special for today and today only. We're going to give you the wife back, but we're taking those girls with us. That is until we can work out a fair trade. I'll even let you set the resolution date. That work?"

Hattie nods slightly.

Davis does the same.

Justin cocks his head birdlike, confused.

Hattie slams the back of her head into the bridge of Justin's nose. His head whips back hard with a crunch of bone and a spray of blood. Hattie shoves Justin's gun arm clear from her head stumbling free toward the car that has her girls.

Davis rages hard at Justin.

Justin spins around like a top, firing wild blasts.

A bullet cuts into Davis's shoulder. Doesn't even slow him down. He crashes into Justin like a runaway train. They bounce off Davis's SUV behind them. Spit flies from Davis's mouth as he grabs a fistful of hair pounding Justin's head into the side of the car. A primal scream leaves his throat as he slams his head over and over again. Indecipherable words pour out from deep inside of him.

Justin jams his fists into Davis's chest pushing him off just enough, creating some space between them, allowing him to squeeze off three shots. All three bullets whiz past Davis as he spins and drops to the gravel. One bullet removes half of the green-eyed beauty's head. Her body slumps, then slides off the trunk to the ground. The other two clunk into the trunk of the BMW.

The gunshots echo, fading quickly into crushing silence.

Hattie screams until the cords in her throat rip. Her children, her babies, are in that trunk. She runs hard toward the car, her eyes zeroed in on the two holes torn into the metal. Tilley grabs her arm, then her hair, pulling her down to the ground. Veins bulge and pop in Hattie's neck as she falls backward.

Davis lands a punch to Justin's jaw then another to his chin. Justin is getting weak, legs giving out. Davis is gaining strength with every punch, knowing every blow is getting him closer to getting to his girls. He grabs Justin's gun hand, gripping it hard, fighting to knock the gun loose. Davis yanks Justin's forearm down with everything he has. There's a crack of bone as his arm tears the rearview mirror off the side of the car. The gun falls to the gravel and Davis manages to kick it free, moving the gun a few feet away from them.

Hattie flips over, jams her palm into Tilley's face, then kicks her in the stomach. Tilley falls back then dives at Hattie as she scrambles in the rocks, moving toward the car.

Justin jams his forearm into Davis's throat. They fall back onto the driveway. Punches miss, then land. Screams and grunts fill the night air. Legs fight for ground, feet skidding in the rocks, each one of them fighting to gain control.

Davis lands a fist to Justin's battered nose, then jams a thumb in his eye. Justin drifts just enough for Davis to shove his hands into Justin's chest knocking him back. Giving him a sliver of space. A chance. Davis pulls himself through the gravel on his hands and knees to the gun. Justin jumps up, racing toward him.

Davis grabs the gun, turns, fires two blasts into Justin's gut. Justin falls backward to the ground, his face pale, shock locked into his eyes. This was not part of the plan. Everything is coming undone. Davis sits up, levels the gun on Justin, then turns the gun toward Tilley and Hattie. They're a mass of twisting, spinning, turning rage. Impossible to get a clear shot.

Justin's hands fumble, finding a large stone. He throws it hard at Davis's head.

Davis fires again, missing to the right, blowing out the window of the SUV. The stone hits Davis in the side of the face. His sight goes white, then returns to a fuzzy version of the world.

Justin is on top of him now, swinging like a man possessed. Justin's fists crash into the side of Davis's head. He can barely see Justin as his vision is fading, failing him. The white is back and taking over his sight quickly. He feels himself slipping away, as if sliding into a warm, milky bath.

Davis raises the gun with everything he has left, firing a blind shot. It cuts harmlessly out toward the stars. Justin slaps the gun to the side. Davis's hand falls limp and the gun slips from his fingers. His consciousness is all but gone. He can only make out shafts of sight through the spots of white that grow and mutate.

Justin has found a much larger stone. It's raised above his head poised to slam down for the kill. His bloody face shines in the moonlight. A demon of the night with a smile on his face, waiting to bring death down on what's left of Davis.

Davis blinks.

"I'm sorry," he whispers. To Hattie. To the girls. Himself.

Justin's body jolts hard, knocked away from Davis. Hattie rolls off to the side of him. The force of her dive sends Justin hard to the right and her rolling into the rocks. Davis's senses slam together, back online if only for a second. His fingers find the gun. Justin pops up.

Davis fires a shot into his chest.

"No!" Tilley screams, racing toward him with a knife in her hand.

Davis turns, firing twice. The shots rip into Tilley, stop her cold, drop her to her knees. Blood spurts and drips from her chest and stomach. She gets to her feet, the knife still in her hand. A cough of blood spits and strings from her lips.

Davis pulls the trigger.

Click.

Hattie drives her foot into Tilley's knee, shoving her aside. Tilley slumps to the ground while Hattie sprints to the car. She bangs on the trunk, screaming for her children to give her a sign. Davis watches while on his knees. Mouth open wide. Listening. Hoping.

Hattie presses her ear to the trunk with arms stretched wide over it. Tears stream, roll and land on the car's steel.

Davis walks toward the car, watching his wife's every move, his body seconds from collapsing. His need to see this through is stronger than the pain. He fights the urge to fall. The urge to give up. To fail.

Hattie talks sweetly into the trunk, her words morphing into a song. Davis's knees shake upon hearing his wife sing softly. He'd watch her sing to their girls every night when they both were only babies in her arms.

There's a thump. A thud mixed with the muffled screams of little girls.

Hattie jumps from the trunk, spinning, looking toward Davis. Their eyes fill, they both breathe again. Davis looks around. He bends down to the green-eyed beauty's lifeless body, searching for the keys to the trunk. He hears the gravel crunch behind him.

"Davis," Hattie says.

Turning, he sees Tilley moving Justin toward the other BMW, his arm over her shoulder. They seem to be carrying one another, like warriors after a battle lost. Their bodies beaten, their wounds seep. Tilley slides Justin into the passenger seat, then braces herself along the car, making it to the driver's side.

Justin clucks his tongue as he shuts the door.

The BMW's engine fires up and the car backs out of the driveway. Leaving.

There's a distant sound of sirens.

Davis finds the keys in the green-eyed beauty's pocket. He tosses them to Hattie then slumps down, sitting in the driveway. Hattie's fingers fumble as she presses down hard on the button to release the trunk.

A bleep. A blink of taillights. The trunk pops open.

The girls pop straight up. Hattie hugs them both as tight as she can while looking them over. Checking, searching for wounds, cuts, anything. They are scared and trembling, but not hurt. Hattie rushes, grabbing the knife from the ground. Fighting the shaking of her hands she cuts the ties free from her girl's wrists.

Davis smiles, then falls over to the side, feeling himself slip back into the warm, milky bath again. This time he doesn't fight it. He closes his eyes, letting himself sink into the abyss. Hearing his family cry, his wife trying to give comfort to their children for the impossible night they've had to endure, Davis catches a last look at them. A snapshot of an image. His family with arms wrapped tight around one another. Safe. A new image to hold on to in his broken brain.

He shuts his eyes.

The world slides away from him.

Darkness slips its fingers into his, leading him far away.

38

———

The grip is loose.

His hold on the here and now is so slight he's not sure if he's even alive.

He's felt movement from time to time. Pin pricks. Voices. Jolts. Lifting, then falling. Flashes of light followed by dark.

He can't remember the last time he opened his eyes, the last time he saw anything outside of his own head. There's little sense of time and space. Life crawls, inching along in complete slush. Then there are moments where he seemingly floats in and out of dreams before slipping into nightmares. All of it jumbled, tangled up with memories of recent days that scratch at the darkness.

He relives his time at the Viceroy hotel bar in Los Angeles. He's been through it many times in his mind. The reality of what happened is replayed like a movie on constant repeat. He's also run through fantasy versions of the same story. Revisionist history versions. He's envisioned one where he walked away the second that Tilley slid into the seat next to him at the bar. There's another version where he never left his room. Stayed there alone watching TV, talking on the phone with his family, then falling asleep. There's a self-serving version too. A fun version. The one where he kicks Justin to the floor, then beats him with a chair. It's become his favorite. Gives him comfort, a feeling of control. Power for the powerless.

"That's cute," Justin says in the darkness.

Davis opens his eyes.

Davis?

An unseen, faraway voice calls his name.

He finds himself lying in the plush bed back in the Viceroy hotel room where he woke up days ago. He's dressed in nothing but the black silk boxers, as he was when he came to in LA. Justin stands above him dressed in his slick, dark suit and red tie, with Tilley standing by his side. She's back to soul-melting seductress. The green-eyed beauty stands by the door with her knife in hand, picking at her nails with the edge of the blade.

Davis?

He hears someone call out again.

"I told you what I was going to do to you," Justin says, playing with Davis's hair. "The first time we met, I told you exactly what I was going to do."

"What?" Davis asks. He remembers Justin saying the same thing at the lake house. "I don't understand."

Davis?

Tilley shakes her head in disappointment before moving toward the dresser. There are two ice cream containers sitting next to the card with Davis's name on it. Davis stares at the ice cream. There's one chocolate, one peanut butter. Tilley takes them both, then exits the room along with the green-eyed beauty.

Davis, please talk to me.

"Justin, I don't understand," Davis says as his panic inches up. "What did you tell me you were going to do?"

"Shhhh. Give it a good think," Justin says, pressing a finger to his lips. "Get some rest, Big Fun. You've had a tough go." He clucks his tongue.

Davis, are you awake?

39

———

Davis jolts awake.

A sharp spike of pain fires through every part of him.

His eyes flutter, blink, struggle to find moisture as they battle to adjust to the harsh light of the room. His tongue feels thick, his mouth dry as a funeral drum. There are odd sounds to the room. Slight, gentle sounds, but mechanical and rhythmic. A series of soft clicks and faint beeps surround him. Annoying and soothing at the same time. The smell of bleach or some sort of industrial-style cleaner burns, filling his nostrils. The world around him feels very still. Stagnant but calm.

Very different from when he was last awake.

As he moves his hands around, his fingertips glide over a set of plastic tubes that run along the side of his arm. Stuck into his arm actually. There's tape holding it all together, connected to something unseen. As his sight starts to come back to him, he can make out an outline of someone standing over him.

Davis?

He pulls back hard, not sure who it is.

"Hey, you decide to come back?" Hattie says.

Davis's eyes dart and dance, searching the room. They were here. He knows they're still here somewhere.

"Where are they?" he asks, his voice shaking.

"Who?"

Davis's head jerks from side to side, scanning the area. He's in a bland-colored box of a room with minimal decoration. A cheap picture in a frame hangs on the wall. A brownish chair. A spattering of flowers sit here and there. The clicking, beeping machines stand on rollers near his bed, flashing the occasional light. He's cloaked in white sheets tucked tight into the bed.

A far cry from the Viceroy.

"I'm in a hospital?" he asks, knowing the answer.

Hattie nods. Her face hangs, bags heavy under her eyes. Looks like she hasn't slept in days.

"Justin, the others. I just saw them. They were here—"

"They're dead, Davis," she says.

"What?"

"I've talked with the police over the last few days and—"

"Days?"

She nods. "State troopers found them on the side of the road a few miles from the lake. They bled out in their car trying to get away, apparently."

Davis can't believe it.

Is it over? Is that possible?

Hattie touches his head, running her fingers through his hair. Like he felt Justin do only moments ago. Davis realizes now that it was Hattie trying to sooth him by playing with his hair. Calling his name. His mind was tricking him, betraying him.

Again.

His arm hangs in some kind of sling. His shoulder is heavily bandaged. He remembers being shot by Justin. The blast echoes in his mind. He still hears it ringing in his ears. The violence, the screams, the thick thumps of fists beating on flesh sound off as if it were happening right now. He lies back down into the bed, grinding his teeth as his head reaches the pillow. Every part of him burns and aches, but none more than what's inside his skull.

Hattie steps back, reaching for the table.

"Sorry. I thought they were here," Davis says, fighting the dryness in his throat.

Hattie holds a cup with a straw in front of his

lips so he can drink. As he sucks down the water he looks at his wife, letting his eyes take her in while the rest of him tries to understand what's happened. She's here. She's been here the whole time. No telling how long she's sat here waiting for him to come to. From the corner of his eye he sees a scattered stack of magazines, an open book by the chair. She's worn out. Her face screams to him how tired she is.

There's something else there, however. He can see that in her face as well. There's a turning of thoughts and feelings going on behind her eyes. Some people might miss it, but to him it's so plainly obvious.

Davis pulls back from the straw. "Thank you."

Hattie nods, taking a step back from the bed and placing the cup back on the table. She swallows hard, as if preparing herself for a conversation she'd rather not have. A talk she never imagined having to have. One no woman wants to have with their husband.

"This is probably not the right time—"

"No, I'm fine."

"You sure?"

He's not, but Davis nods anyway.

"The police told me everything. What Justin did. What he does." Hattie looks down. "What he did to you."

Davis chews on the inside of his mouth. An

odd feeling of relief creeps over him. It's all out in the open now, finally. Facts that he's tried so hard to keep away from her are now exposed. For better or worse.

"I saw the pictures too," she says.

"Those weren't real." Davis sits up fast, ignoring the pain. "They staged all that to get to me—"

"I know." She gently helps him lie back down. "Why?" Hattie asks, adjusting his pillow. "Why didn't you tell me what was happening?"

"I had to handle it."

"Davis, come on."

"I did what I thought was best."

"By not telling me anything?"

"It's the truth. I was trying to protect you."

"Oh?" She stops herself from what she's about to say. Her face has shifted to red. She takes a deep breath. "All that was for my benefit?"

"Hattie—"

"It's not the pictures, Davis. The police looked at everything. I know about the money problems you hid from me too. I know about how bad things got with the business. The meetings that went wrong. You moving money around in secret behind my back. You made up that story about us needing to go to the lake without putting any thought or concern into what might happen to me. To the girls."

"How are they? Where are the girls?"

"They're okay. Far from perfect, but okay considering."

Davis looks away, staring at a corner of the room.

"I thought... I thought I was doing the right thing."

"That wasn't your decision to make. Not alone, Davis." She shakes her head, working it through while speaking. "You didn't even give us a chance to try and work it out. Nothing. You didn't tell me anything but the bullshit stories you decided to feed me."

"I didn't know what to do."

"You lied to me."

"What was I supposed to do?"

"You talk to your wife. You tell your wife what the hell is going on."

Davis turns away, knowing everything she's saying is true.

"What are we supposed to do now?" she asks, almost pleading for an answer she knows doesn't exist. "Pretend that everything's fine? Oh great, the bad guys are dead, so we just move on like none of that happened?"

Hattie's eyes bore through Davis. It's that look, the one that's come up in the last few days, the one he never wanted or wants to see again. Now it's commonplace.

Davis hears Justin's words rattle in his head. The words he said that violent night in the lake house driveway. He said he told Davis when they first met what he was going to do.

"I don't know that I can flip a switch and go back," Hattie says.

Davis's mind fumbles for the words Justin said that night at the hotel bar.

Trust is the main thing. You spend a lifetime building it and can lose it in the blink of an eye.

"How do I believe what you say to me now?" Hattie asks, tears forming.

If you remove the trust between people, there's nothing to hold on to. Don't you agree?

"How am I supposed to trust anything you say?"

A cold rush rises up through Davis. He stares lifelessly at his wife. Justin told him what he was going to do—make Davis destroy the trust between him and his family. Something that can't be repaired or restored by money.

"Your brother and sister are here. They'll help you get home once the doctors say it's okay." She wipes her eyes with the back of her hand. "I'm taking the girls to my parents for a while."

Davis nods. "For how long?" he barely gets out.

"Not sure. I need... I need some time."

"Can I see them?"

"This has been hard on them, Davis. Real hard. They cry during the day, they have nightmares."

Realizing he's the reason for the pain he's caused his wife and his children, an enormous weight of sadness hits him, crushing down on him like a piano dropped from above.

"You've been out for a couple of days. They didn't like seeing you like this," Hattie says. "They said their goodbyes last night. They drew you some cards. They're over there."

Davis glances toward a roller table by the bed. Next to the water pitcher are two folded pieces of paper with crayon drawings sprawled across them. Bright, wonderful colors were used with great care to create words like *Daddy*, *Get Better* and *Love*.

"Hattie," Davis says, his voice cracking, "I understand, but you can't. This is what he wanted to happen. You're giving him exactly what he wanted."

"Who?"

"Justin."

"Davis, that—"

"He wanted this to happen. This was his whole plan."

"His plan was about money. Period."

"Yes, of course it was about money. But destroying us is what he was doing for fun. To amuse himself. It was like entertainment to him. You can't let him win."

Hattie looks at him. Eyes hard. Completely stripped of feelings. "I can't believe you."

"It's true. Please don't do—"

"I didn't do a damn thing. You did."

Davis slips back into the pillow, mouth open, nothing to say.

"I gotta go," Hattie says. As she reaches the door, she stops. "I talked to the company, the money manager. They're not happy with the bad press, but they're still honoring the purchase agreement. Not sure they could get out of it even if they wanted to."

"Hattie—"

"Congratulations, we're rich."

She leaves the room.

40

THE WEEKS after the hospital weren't easy.

The long hours of rehab.

The endless regimen of medications.

The nights void of sleep.

The therapist has helped Davis in a lot of ways. It took a few visits for him to buy into the process, to get comfortable with the idea of talking with her about everything. Not something that has ever come naturally for him, but he's made some respectable progress recently. Unwinding the work of Justin and friends was first. It was difficult, hard work, but they've managed to untangle some other less obvious issues that have plagued Davis for a long time as well. Things he didn't even know he was hanging on to.

His brother and sister have been good to him. A level of kindness and understanding he never imagined possible from them. They don't ask a lot of questions, letting him tell them things when he wants to talk. As his strength has returned, they have been coming around less and less.

The emptiness of the house is starting to weigh on him now. The open space seems endless.

As the number of pain meds he's been taking becomes fewer, his feelings are becoming more unavoidable. Less numb than before. He hears his girls playing in the house when they aren't there. He smells the smells of meals they've shared. He thinks of when he and Hattie bought this house. Choosing the things they needed, deciding where those things would go. Weighing what they could afford and the lively discussion about the things they could not.

He shakes his head, thinking of arguments over nothing, letting the water rinse away the soap from his healing body. As he steps out from the shower, he carefully pats dry the healing wound on his shoulder with a towel. The cuts and scrapes have all but healed, but the mark from a gunshot to the shoulder is going to be there forever.

A parting gift from Justin. A constant reminder.

Davis stands in the closet staring at the choices that hang in front of him. He selects a shirt—she never liked that one—chooses another, then another. He remembers Hattie said he looked good in that one.

He'd ask the girls what they thought, if they were here.

He had a meeting with an attorney and an accountant about a week ago. A long meeting to go over everything. He's had a few calls with them before, but the meeting in person was the big one. It was the first time Davis felt strong enough to talk about it. All of it. They went over the sale of the company, the finer deal points, and all the final paperwork dealing with Todd's death.

Todd's death.

When the attorney said those words, Davis wanted to run from the room. Instead, Davis sat stone-faced during most of the meeting, listening to all the work that had been done without his knowledge or his input. A mixed bag of emotions if ever there was one. Sadness, anger, regret all packed up nice and neat. He held it all back, held on to it all while he was there, but when he got home after that meeting he let it all go.

It happened the second he shut the door and set down his keys and papers from the lawyers. If he was being honest, it happened when he noticed the dog wasn't even there. The dog that greeted him usually before anyone else. The girls wanted him with them. In the silence of the house, his feelings came roaring out, could not be stopped this time, flooding out in tears, beating on walls, followed by time sitting quietly in the dark thinking. Everything he needed to let go of ever since LA, and even before, was released and set free from inside of him.

Davis gets into the car, backs out of the driveway. The Pixies play on his way to the restaurant in downtown Portland. A place Hattie always talked about going to. A trendy sushi place he'd always said he'd take her to, but never did.

He arrives at the restaurant a few minutes early, wanting to be there before she gets there. He thought of buying flowers, but thought it would be too much. He toys with the idea of having a whiskey at the bar to loosen up, but thinks better of it. Even allows himself to snicker at the thought. *Must be getting better*, he thinks.

Checking his phone for the third time, he breathes in deep. She's late. He taps the edge of the phone on the table.

Did she reconsider? Can't blame her. Who wouldn't?

The waiter checks on him again, asking if he's sure he wouldn't like a drink from the bar. He says he's fine.

The minutes crawl.

He thinks about texting her, maybe calling her, but stops himself.

A woman and man enter and sit at the table

next to Davis. They're young. The guy's nervous. So is she. They exchange awkward comments about how nice the place is. He gives a joke that falls flat. She laughs like it was the funniest thing ever. He tries not to let his eyes bug out when he sees the prices.

Davis smiles, remembering his first date with Hattie.

He checks his phone again.

She's not coming. It's too soon.

Maybe we'll try again, he tells himself.

Davis tries to get the waiter's attention, already thinking of an excuse to give him.

Hattie turns the corner. Sight of her starts a flutter in his stomach. He smiles to himself; he's as nervous as the kid next to him.

Hattie turns, sees him seated in the back.

They lock eyes.

Davis bites his lower lip.

Hattie cracks a smile.

THANK YOU!

Thank you so much for reading Relentless. Hope you enjoyed the ride. I occasionally send newsletters with details about new books, special offers, and other fun stuff. If you join my Reader's Group you get all that plus 3 free short stories. Who doesn't love free reads?

Just visit www.mikemccrary.com and you'll get all that plus more. Hope to see you there.

Mike

ACKNOWLEDGMENTS

I say the same thing with each book and I will continue saying it until it stops being true. You can't do a damn thing alone, so I'd like to thank the people who gave help and hope during this fun and self-loathing little writing life of mine.

The list of those people is insanely long and keeps growing by the day. The idea of leaving someone out and listening to them bitch later is a little more than I can take on right now, but I'll point out a couple.

I would like to pass along a special thank you to Sean Platt. If not for Sean this book would not have happened. Period. From idea to developement, Sean was huge. So, thanks Sean as well as the amazing people of Sterling & Stone.

Thanks to the fine folks that hang out with me at Bcon. You've saved me from giving up on more than one occation. Thanks to the editors and keepers of the faith, Elizabeth A. White and J. David Osborne. Johnny Shaw, Jammie Mason, Mathew Fitzsimmons, and Scott Montgomery for listening to me whine and bitch during this book and others. Let's just go on to say I am very thankful to all of you who've been a part of this writer thing. I am truly grateful to those people who have helped me out and talked me off the ledge more times than I can count. This is me being honest, no bullshit here. Hopefully you know who you are.

Also, if you're reading this right now you deserve a big-ass thank you from me as well. Even if we've never met, you've been cool and kind enough to grab a copy of my book and give it a read and that, my dear friendly readers, deserves the biggest ACKNOWLEDGEMENT of them all.

Thanks, good people.

ABOUT THE AUTHOR

Mike has been a waiter, securities trader, dishwasher, investment manager, and an unpaid Hollywood intern. He's quit corporate America, come back, been fired, been promoted, been fired, and currently, from his home in Texas, he writes stories about questionable people making questionable decisions.

Keep up with Mike at...
www.mikemccrary.com
mccrarynews@mikemccrary.com